ALSO BY MICHAEL NEWTON

Gideon Thorn

Skinwalker

Leviathan Rising

Ghost Town

Mountain Devils

Soul Slayers

Hallowed Ground

Night Flyers

EMPTY GRAVES

EMPTY GRAVES

A WEIRD WESTERN

GIDEON THORN
BOOK 8

MICHAEL NEWTON

Empty Graves
Paperback Edition

Dark Wolf Books
An Imprint of Wolfpack Publishing
1707 E. Diana Street
Tampa, FL 33610

www.darkwolfbooks.com

Paperback ISBN 979-8-89567-609-7
Ebook ISBN 979-8-89567-608-0

EMPTY GRAVES

PROLOGUE

LAKE BOGGY BAYOU, ARKANSAS: MARCH 11, 1877

Asa Daughtrey made his living as a game poacher and scofflaw, one of countless others hunting day and night around Chicot County, where southeast Arkansas shoved up against the Mississippi River, with Louisiana just a few miles farther south. He lived alone, inside a marshland shack, acquiring whatever he needed—flour, salt, a woman now and then—on rare trips to the county seat at Lake Village.

Mostly, he prowled the land, tracking and killing anything that swam, crawled, ran or flew. Asa consumed most of that prey himself, but made his pocket money selling pelts, spare meat, and certain curiosities like skulls and such to anyone with ready cash in hand. One of his better customers craved fancy feathers for a manufacturer of ladies' hats, down in New Orleans—or was it New York?

Asa couldn't care less, as long as he got paid.

Today, though, he was after alligators.

Asa mainly caught gators on big old baited hooks, then shot them in the brain pan before getting busy with his skinning knife. Those hides went to New York—no doubt about it in his mind, this time—while Daughtrey boiled the heads down to clean skulls and sold them off as novelties. As for the meat—an average twelve-footer generally tipped the scales around eight hundred pounds—he kept most of it, using what he couldn't eat as bait for fish or smaller animals.

That was the only life he knew, and you would never catch him trying to raise crops, backbreaking labor from sunup to dusk on soggy land the swamp was always trying to reclaim.

He'd come well-armed for it today, packing the Fayetteville Rifle he'd carried during the late War of Northern Aggression, using it to kill blue-bellies at Pea Ridge in March of 1862, after he'd joined the so-called Army of the West to fight for Dixie's freedom. After that, he'd fought at Chickasaw Bayou and Vicksburg, and finally at Helena, where Yankees overran the boys in butternut on Independence Day. Union soldiers occupied the whole of Arkansas a little after that, and Asa Daughtrey made it home by hook or crook to whatever was left.

One thing he'd brought along, not what he called stealing, had been the .58-caliber musket manufactured in North Carolina, copied almost exactly from the Union's Springfield Model 1861, weighing twelve pounds, just a trifle under fifty inches long. It was a muzzle-loader and fired Minié balls with a maximum effective range of 500 yards, despite sights calibrated out to 800.

Asa's backup weapon, in peace as in war, was a Beaumont-Adams revolver, imported from England by both sides in the war. It was another muzzle-loader, .442-

caliber, with a nifty double-action trigger mechanism that the Brits called "self-cocking." All that meant was that a simple trigger-pull would fire it, and you didn't have to thumb the hammer back before each shot like Mr. Colt's designs.

Daughtrey had killed both men and animals with each of his two guns, though only one man since he'd come home from the war. Some kind of damned game warden, he had been, a carpetbagging busy-body who thought he could throw his weight around, tell decent white men where and what to hunt, as if he owned the goddamned world.

He'd made fair bait, and nobody on Earth would ever find him now, not even if they started sieving gator shit.

Today, poling along the brackish waterway, Asa saw many things he could've slain for food or profit if he'd had a mind to: feral hogs, raccoons, possums, mallards and whooping cranes, green herons, and a red-tailed hawk. If he'd been fishing, he could easily have hooked a catfish for his supper, maybe bass, trout, or a smaller crappie. Other things he didn't mess with, like the cottonmouths that lay in wait for careless hikers, or the ruby-throated hummingbirds that always made him smile.

Today, he only wanted gator, and his hook was baited, not with game warden, but with leftovers from the last scaly behemoth he had bagged. Did using gator meat for gator bait mean he encouraged cannibalism? And so what if he did? Big gators fed on smaller gators all the time, along with snakes, turtles, whatever else came within reach of their tremendous jaws. He'd seen one take a panther, not too long after the war, and he was smart enough to make sure no big bastard added Asa Daughtrey to its menu.

Now, if he could only find one large enough to make the trip worthwhile, and then entice it with his hook...

A swirl of murky water in among the reeds ahead, off to his left, made Asa think this was his lucky day. He let the current draw his skiff in that direction, rifle braced across his knees, revolver tucked under his belt, the hook and bait lying on sackcloth down between his feet, attached to twenty feet of chain.

Once Asa hooked a gator, it could fight, but it would never get away.

Closer to shore, he swept the rushes with keen eyes, seeking a gator hole that meant an underwater lair, someplace to set his bait. Instead, another bubbling swirl of water captured his attention, and his mind could hardly grasp what he saw next.

It was a man—or, rather, *used* to be one, obviously dead now, driven to the surface by the gases that build up inside a decomposing corpse. Covered with mud and algae from the water, it was bobbing there, its head and shoulders visible at first, then slipping back, and now resurfacing.

He wondered if the poor dead bastard had once been a hunter like himself, who'd overreached and wound up staying there instead of taking home a prize. It happened all too frequently to men less cautious than Daughtrey, and all it meant to Asa was less competition when he took his kills to town.

"Tough luck, old man," he told the dead thing—then recoiled and nearly fell out of his boat when its eyes opened wide.

"Jesus, the fuckin' hell!" he blurted out, then managed to collect himself and ask, hating the way his voice shivered, "Is you awright?"

That was a stupid question, Daughtrey realized. Whatever else this character might be, *all right* wasn't an option. But it got a kind of answer, anyway, the almost-dead man opening his mouth—there went a worm of some kind, wriggling out—and sort of growled at him.

Asa recoiled again, then figured he might not have any voice to speak of, or speak *with,* if he'd come close to drowning in the swamp, inhaling moss and worms and all. It was a wonder this joker could breathe and move at all.

More of a wonder when he suddenly surged forward, hard eyes boring into Daughtrey's, as its bloated, wrinkled hands clutched at the port-side gunwale of his skiff.

And why was he still snarling like some kind of hungry animal?

"Let go a that, ya crazy bastard!" Asa shouted at his weird assailant, thumping him a good one with the musket's barrel, opening the rotten-smelling stranger's scalp.

Blood should've spurted from a wound like that, but what he saw instead was brownish ooze, not all that different from bayou water. Startled, Asa cocked his weapon, aimed it at the target's sunken chest beneath a tattered shirt, and fired without warning.

A blind man couldn't miss at that range, muzzle almost pressed against the swamp man's chest, and Daughtrey *saw* the hole made by his Minié ball, more than a half-inch in diameter. It should've been an instant kill, spewing heart's blood, but nothing spilled out of the wound except more of the greasy-looking fluid that still trickled from his adversary's scalp.

And the damned man or *thing* was still growling at him, baring decayed and broken teeth stained by tobacco or the bayou's muck.

With no time to reload his long gun, Asa dropped it in

the skiff beside his gator hook and ripped the six-gun from his belt. A gaping chest wound might not stop the lunatic, but he'd be shit out of tomorrows once six bullets blew his skull apart.

"You've had it now, man!" Asa blurted, rapid-firing—just as other hands clamped on his shoulders from behind, and dragged him from his boat, pulling him down and down into the endless dark.

ONE

CHICOT COUNTY, ARKANSAS: MARCH 13, 1877

The trip by train to Little Rock, from Tucson in the Arizona Territory, had conveyed Gideon Thorn across the better part of thirteen hundred miles in four days' time.

A northern railroad could've made the journey quicker —back in June, the Transcontinental Express had spanned America from New York City to San Francisco in just eighty-three hours—but war damage and shabby materials slowed things considerably down below the Mason-Dixon Line, where locomotives nearly split their seams rolling at twenty miles per hour. Add in two stops where he'd had to switch trains with his animals, in El Paso and Dallas, plus a slew of shorter whistle stops along the way, and Thorn was straining at the leash when he had finally debarked at Little Rock's Union Station.

All the way, he had been reading and rereading the last telegram that he'd received in Arizona, till he had it memorized.

> BOSTON: OBI MAGORO SENDS—HOPE ALL IS WELL. HAVE WORD FROM CHICOT COUNTY, ARKANSAS, OF DINAH PILCHER. WORKING ON A STORY THERE SAID TO BE "STRANGE," NOW MISSING. NO CONTACT WITH COUNTY SHERIFF OR EDITOR OF "LAKE SHORE SENTINEL" NEWSPAPER SAID TO BE COLLABORATING WITH HER. LEAVING IT TO YOUR DISCRETION FOR INVESTIGATION. O. M.

Obi was Gideon's best friend and mentor, presently the sole surviving occupant of the Thorn family's mansion, standing among others of its kind on Boston's stately Beacon Hill. And he was certainly the only African residing in the neighborhood, unless you counted liveried domestics living at the beck and call of Brahmin masters.

Dinah Pilcher was the lady journalist who'd come into Thorn's life while he was tracking an apocalyptic cult that practiced human sacrifice in California's San Diego County. She had barely come through that alive, but it had opened up her eyes to possibilities beyond the former scope of her imagination, and she'd joined him later for a job in Colorado, where he'd evened up an ancient family score.

And after that...well, their relationship was complicated. She'd hoped to publish an account of Thorn's odyssey through the West, pursuing mysteries that boggled mundane minds and sometimes ended lives. They'd traveled for a while together after Colorado, she had taken notes galore and talked about a book—or maybe more than one—recounting Gideon's exploits. Along the way, they'd sometimes shared a bed, and he'd enjoyed that very much, but then they'd parted company, her choice, declaring that she couldn't work forever on the road.

And now, it seemed, she had followed another road to trouble, possibly the last trip she would ever take.

Thorn didn't want to think about that, but he'd seen and done too much during his past four years or so of traveling to cherish any fantasies about a happy ending when a talented and strong-willed woman disappeared, chasing a mystery.

What *kind* of mystery?

That question made him spend a precious day in Little Rock, poring over recent back issues of the *Arkansas State Gazette*. Aside from learning that the state seemed prone to bloody feuds involving race and politics, the only thing he learned had come from two short articles from Chicot County, speculating on the ghouls responsible for robbing graves.

The *State Gazette* put "ghouls" inside quotation marks, clearly suggesting some sick humans at the root of it. Gideon knew that he would have to wait and see.

Off-hand, he understood that robbing graves was not particularly rare, as crimes went, either in America or in Europe. Anatomists required corpses for the instruction of new doctors, and for research into causes of disease. In most Western nations, laws limited their acquisitions to a few people who willed their bodies to a hospital or university, plus convicts who were hanged or died in prison by some other means, with no known next of kin to cart off their remains. Under those rules, "resurrection men" sometimes stepped in to fill the gap and profited thereby.

The most infamous case that came to mind had been recorded back in 1828—nearly a quarter-century before Gideon's birth—in Edinburgh, Scotland. Two resurrection men named William Burke and William Hare supplied fresh corpses to physician Robert Knox, a Fellow of the Royal Society of Edinburgh. Knox always needed more and paid top dollar, so the grave-robbers had tried a shortcut, killing thirteen victims by a means of suffocation later nicknamed "Burking."

Burke was hanged—and then, ironically, dissected as a specimen at Edinburgh Hospital, his skeleton preserved on permanent display. Hare served a year in prison for peddling the dead, and Knox walked free, although a mob attacked his home, prompting a swift retreat to London. There, his reputation made him unemployable until he found work as a pathologist at the city's Free Cancer Hospital, performing autopsies.

And in the meantime, Edinburgh's scandal had become a children's rhyme:

Up the close and doon the stair,
But and ben' wi' Burke and Hare.
Burke's the butcher, Hare's the thief,
Knox the boy that buys the beef.

More recently, in 1848 and '49, several graves had been opened at Montparnasse Cemetery in Paris, the corpses grossly mutilated, till a cemetery watchman set a booby trap and wounded Sergeant François Bertrand of the French Army, who'd confessed to sexually assaulting lifeless men and women alike, before he gutted and dismembered them. Reporters dubbed him the "Montparnasse Vampire," and Belgian psychiatrist Joseph Guislain had coined a term for Bertrand's mental illness: necrophilia. After all that, the sergeant only served one year in prison, moving on from there to hold jobs as a postman and a lighthouse keeper.

Now, were similar offenses happening in southeastern Arkansas, or was it *something else*?

From Little Rock, Thorn had a choice of traveling 130 miles on horseback to the Chicot County seat at Lake Village, taking the best part of another week, or traveling again by train. He'd opted for the rails, which meant crossing the Mississippi River to Greenville, covering 150 miles in roughly eight hours. He'd spent the night there, then set out this morning—Tuesday—riding back toward Arkansas on his gray stallion, Shadow, with his molly pack mule Belle trailing behind.

That trip was twenty-one miles long, but naturally, there was no bridge over the great river separating Mississippi from Thorn's goal. That meant waiting for a hung-over, unwashed ferryman to welcome seven other people, one more horse, and a disgruntled hog aboard his creaky boat and slowly cross the water drawn by stout lines anchored on the other side.

Amidst that motley crew, Gideon was a striking figure: six foot four at twenty-five years old, weighing 170 pounds. He dressed all in black, from his flat-brimmed had to frock coat, pants, and knee-high boots; the only variation was his white shirt, set off with a black string tie. Even his hair was black, although it had a white streak down its center part, concealed by his headgear from fellow travelers.

And just as well, because he didn't need them gawping at him, and if anyone had asked about it, they'd have been bemused by his reply: a childhood scar, etched by a talon of the same beast that had massacred his parents and his older brother at their cabin on the east slope of the Rocky Mountains, back when Thorn was barely two years old.

This morning, as it happened, other ferry passengers were busy staring at Thorn's weaponry. Around his waist, he wore twin Colt Peacemakers, with a Bowie knife around in back. His frock coat covered some of that, but anyone could see the haft of a short dagger, visible above its sheath in his right boot. Thorn also carried two long guns. A Winchester Model 1873 lever-action, chambered for the same .44-40 rounds as his pistols, resided in a saddle boot aboard Shadow. The other—an 1872 Sharps rifle chambered in .50-90 caliber, sporting a long custom-made telescopic sight atop its thirty-two-inch—traveled in a buckskin wrap, as part of Belle's load for the trail.

Using its scope, the Sharps could strike a target from one thousand yards, although the manufacturer judged its "effective" range at half that distance. It was a single-shot breech-loading gun, but an experienced marksman like Gideon could manage eight to ten shots in a minute's time, at need.

Thorn didn't plan on shooting anyone or anything today, but it was still early. And once he'd reached his destination, when he found out what ill fate had lain in store for Dinah Pilcher...then all bets were off.

Thorn knew that Dinah was a strong, resourceful woman who could take care of herself in most perilous situations. He had seen that for himself, six months ago in Colorado, when she'd fought with him and with Obi Magoro to destroy the beast that, Thorn suspected, had wiped out his family. All that was true, but Thorn knew there were other circumstances, other possibilities for danger, that Dinah hadn't encountered or imagined yet.

Whether that danger came from humans, animals, or something from the supernatural, Thorn knew *he* hadn't seen it all, and Dinah, relatively speaking, was a novice next to Gideon.

For all Thorn knew, he might be riding to his death. But if it came to that, at least he'd go down trying to recover—or avenge—a friend and former lover. Anyone who tried to put him off that trail was risking major injury or death.

During the ferry ride, Thorn used his mind to calm Shadow's and Belle's uneasiness at traveling across the broad, deep Mississippi on a boat that lurched and grumbled to itself while listing slightly to starboard. Communicating mentally with certain animals—excluding birds, for some reason he didn't grasp—was a strange talent Thorn had cultivated from his childhood, starting at the orphanage in Lawrence, Kansas, where he'd landed following the massacre that left him without any living relatives he knew. After it marked him as a "freak" to bullies at the so-called children's home, Thorn learned to keep his talent hidden, under cover, using it when no one else suspected or could pick up on its signs.

He had escaped the orphanage because his last surviving kin—an aunt, Drusilla Thorn—had learned belatedly about the slaughter of her brother Aaron, Gideon's father, together with his wife Felicity and older son Thomas. A negligent sheriff in Colorado, then a part of Kansas Territory, blamed the killings on a grizzly that forgot to hibernate over the winter, and gave up trying to find the beast upon deciding it was too damned cold to mount a search.

As luck or Fate would have it, Aunt Drusilla was the dead-end of a wealthy line, small but imposing at five foot three and barely one hundred pounds soaking wet. Part of her strength derived from forceful personality, the rest from her late father's vast fortune, left to her with the Boston mansion at his death. As a young man in business, Russell Thorn seemed to possess the Midas Touch, retiring early while his money reproduced itself under the stewardship of watchful Messrs. Block, Enright & Sloan. He'd traveled the world in search of high adventure, leaving daughter Drusilla—who'd lost her mother at age twelve—mostly to raise herself with aid from pricey chaperons and tutors till she didn't need them anymore.

On one such trip, to Africa, Drusilla's father had collected a peculiar souvenir: Obi Magoro, brought back home to the mansion on Pinckney Street as Russell's servant, later acting in the same capacity for Miss Thorn when her father died, adding selfless protector to his list of tasks. Drusilla never married, fending off the gold-diggers who sought her hand and fortune, until one day in the latter part of 1854, she'd heard the ghastly news of Aaron's family and sent Obi Magoro westward to retrieve her young nephew.

She'd put Gideon through Waverly Academy, a high-priced school where older boys, like those before them at the Kansas orphanage, amused themselves by picking on the new kid. That ended when Obi started teaching Thorn the martial arts of his West African homeland: Dambe bare-knuckle boxing, Engolo ritual combat, and Nguni stick-fighting. The next few bullies bled, then learned to go in search of other prey, until Thorn offered his protection to their weaker classmates and discovered they could be his friends.

From Waverly, Drusilla paid Thorn's way through Harvard University, where he studied "liberal arts," including anthropology and history; biology, botany, and zoology; classical literature and comparative religions. Graduating with a bachelor's degree in 1873, Gideon planned on Harvard Law, but first accepted Aunt Drusilla's gift of a summer abroad in Europe. Her death had cut that short and brought him home as heir to the entire fortune, with a proviso that Obi Magoro should remain on Beacon Hill.

Thorn was delighted and wouldn't have had it any other way.

With sudden, almost boundless wealth at his disposal, Gideon had first deferred, then given up on studying the law. Instead, he wanted *answers*: first, about the slayings of his parents and his brother; beyond that, solutions to a long list of life's other mysteries.

His Aunt Drusilla, an extremely competent businesswoman, was also an ardent occultist and Spiritualist, a personal acquaintance of Paschal Beverly Randolph, renowned practitioner of tarot cards and ouija boards. She'd hosted séances on Beacon Hill, involving Gideon when he was old enough to understand, and while that penchant made established preachers look askance at her, Gideon knew from private observation that her good works, charity, and personal morality outshone those of her whispering critics.

Thorn, never one for organized religion, had reviewed the major faiths, adopting anything of use they had to teach him, while discarding cant and bigotry. Around his neck, beneath his shirt and tie, a silver chain supported symbols of assorted faiths: a small cross, Star of David, crescent moon of Islam, pentagram of paganism, and a feather representing Native American beliefs. He had found value in them all but let none dominate him or divert him from what he regarded as his life's calling.

That journey had taken him across the continent, solving some crimes of human origin that baffled lawmen, other times confronting entities that "normal" men—if they believed in them at all—might label ghosts or monsters. Earlier this very month, in Arizona Territory, he'd destroyed a nest of creatures engineered by a demented scientist and raised to feed on blood—whether from people or their livestock had been immaterial to their creator.

Overall, Thorn would have been hard pressed to say whether the acts of men, of beasts, or otherworldly spirits posed a greater danger to what most people defined as "civilized" society. In fact, he sometimes wondered whether it was civilized at all, or ever could be by the individuals who schemed to place themselves in charge.

But Dinah Pilcher had been pure, as much as anyone could be these days.

And damn it, he was sickened, thinking of her in the past tense, as if she were absolutely dead and gone.

"Missing," Obi Magoro's telegram had specified, while working on a "strange" story in Arkansas. That made it something up Gideon's line, and he was eaten up guilt at having treated Dinah to a glimpse of his world in the first place. Without that introduction, might she not be safe and happy back in San Diego now?

But, no, that wasn't true. They'd met while separately looking into one of Thorn's "typical" cases: murders marked by mutilation that propelled them both into collision with a cult that aimed for nothing less than the obliteration of humanity, sparing only the sect's tiny circle of followers.

Without Dinah, they might well have succeeded, and she had come back for more later, in Colorado, once again placing her own life on the line. Gideon couldn't blame himself for that. Without the curiosity and willfulness that led her into danger, she'd have been a wholly different person. They'd never have met or shared so much.

But which was worse: to meet, admire, then lose someone, or never to have known them in the first place? Carry that thought to its logical conclusion: knowing that all men must die, some of them through great suffering, would it be "better" if they'd never tasted life at all?

Thorn couldn't answer that question for anyone except himself, and his reply was negative. Given a choice, he'd always take the risk and hazard its outcome, rather than sitting idly in a room somewhere back east, counting his money in a musty house devoid of memories.

And when Death found him, as it overtook all humans, he would know that he had done his best from start to finish off the race.

But now Thorn was pushing five hours since he'd left Greenville, and he still hadn't seen a sign for Lake Village along the road that he'd been following. His only consolation was that—on his map, at least—it seemed to be the only road serving Lake Village from the east.

He lightly tested Belle and Shadow once again. The stallion seemed at ease, not tired from traveling so far; the mule plodded along, eyeing the countryside and wondering when they would stop to let her graze.

"Not long, Belle," Thorn replied aloud. "Can't be much farther now."

As if in answer to his spoken words, Gideon saw a small sign up ahead, facing in his direction on the dirt road's right-hand side. It read: LAKE VILLAGE, 2 MILES.

They had covered roughly half that distance, picking up the pace, before Gideon topped a low rise and saw four riders spread out across the road. Two faced in his direction, toward the east, their comrades gazing off to westward, where Lake Village lay, still out of sight.

As soon as Thorn came into view, one of the horsemen facing him said something to the rest, and those who'd had their backs toward him reversed their horses, so that all four had him covered.

"Well," Thorn told his animals. "Can't say I like the looks of this bunch."

All of them were armed, with pistols on their belts and long guns in their saddle boots, though none of them had drawn a weapon yet. One of them, presumably their leader, raised an empty hand—either in greeting or a vague gesture for Gideon to halt—then let it drop again.

Thorn didn't buy the notion of a quarantine surrounding Chicot County's seat of government. If there were any active epidemic in the neighborhood, that surely would've made it to the pages of the *State Gazette*. Which meant the riders blocking him from further progress must be highwaymen.

And if he turned back now, tried cutting through the woods to blaze his own trail westward, would they follow him? Were others waiting out of sight, among the trees, right now?

Thorn's talent for silent communication between minds had no impact on humans, just as it was lost on birds. He'd pondered that at length, and finally just learned to live with it. Scanning the woods to either side of him, he saw no one trying to hide there, but he couldn't prove a negative, either.

If he was bound to face these strangers, whether four or more, Thorn chose to do it on the rural highway's open ground.

First thing, though, he touched base with Belle and

Shadow, asking both if they were game to go ahead. Shadow seemed almost eager; Belle responded with the kind of mental shrug that seemed to say, "Just get it done."

"All right, then," Thorn said, as he looped the stallion's reins loosely around his saddle horn. Next, he released the hammer thongs that held his twin Colts snug inside their holsters. Finally, hands resting on his thighs, Gideon gave Shadow his head and muttered, "Here we go."

TWO

"Well, howdy, pilgrim," said the mouthpiece for the highwaymen, when Thorn was near enough to hear him speaking in a normal tone. "How be's you this fine day?"

"Depends on how it goes from here, I guess," Thorn said.

The gunman—slender almost to emaciation, having gone at least three days without a shave, and longer still since any of his clothes were washed—blinked once, maybe surprised by Thorn's reply, then put some extra candlepower in his smile.

"Expectin' trouble, are you?"

"Every minute of my day," said Gideon.

The leader looked around, exchanging sidelong glances with his men, then nodded as his head swung back toward Thorn. "That's mighty wise for strangers passin' through these parts. Do I detect a bit of Yankee in your voice, Mister?"

"Kansas, by way of Massachusetts." Thorn saw no reason to try and hide it, thereby simply looking foolish.

"Yep. I'd say that's Yankee to the core, awright."

"Well, now we've settled that," Thorn said, "if you'll just ease aside and let me pass..."

"To where, exac'ly, friend?"

"Are we friends?" Thorn inquired.

"Well, I ain't sure. But truth be told, I've started wonderin' myself. What you think?"

"For a start," Thorn said, "all of my friends know my name, just as I know theirs. I don't remember ever meeting you before."

"That is a fact, pilgrim. But maybe you've still heard of us. The name's Wakefield."

Thorn frowned. "One name for all of you?"

"That be's the *fambly* name. We all got *Christian* names, o' course."

"And are you Christians, Mr. Wakefield?"

That earned Gideon another blink. The leader's sunken cheeks were coloring a bit, beneath his weathered tan. "Well, Jesus, what 'n hell else would we be?"

"I had to ask," Thorn said. "Where I come from, the proper Christians don't block public highways, stopping random travelers."

"No? Well, remember you're in Arkansas, not up in Massy-chu-setts, yeah?"

"So, you're a different kind of Christian down here, then?"

"Mister, it ain't the smartest thing you ever done, bad-mouthin' someone else's church."

"Which church is that, if you don't mind me asking? I might like to come around on Sunday morning, thank your pastor for the Christian hospitality of his parishioners."

"You tryin' to be smart?" the leading Wakefield challenged.

"My intelligence is not a recent acquisition. I've been working up to it for years."

One of the others finally chimed in, asking their point man, "What 'n hell's he sayin, Bert?"

"Shut up, Randy!" Bert snapped. And then, to Thorn, "You wouldn't be another goddamn carpetbagger comin' down to throw your weight around, by any chance?"

Thorn cocked a thumb over his shoulder, toward Belle's load. "You see a carpetbag back there?"

"I wanna know exac'ly where you're goin', Mister Massy-chu-setts."

"See, you got my name wrong, so I guess we aren't friends after all."

"Answer the damned question!"

"Not that it's any of your business, Bert, but I'm bound for Lake Village. And you're still blocking the road."

Ignoring that, Bert asked him, "Who you gonna see in Lake Village?"

"Anyone who's there," Thorn told him. "Starting with the county sheriff."

Wakefield barked a laugh at that, his kinfolk joining in as if it were required. "Old Ethan Mallory? That tub o' guts?"

"I couldn't say, not having met him yet. But when I do, I'll give him your regards."

"He knows what all us Wakefields think a him, already."

"No love lost, I take it?"

"What you need to think about just now, is whether you'll be gettin' through to him or not."

"Now, that sounds like a threat."

"Maybe you ain't as dumb as I surmised. I like that stallion, so I'll have 'im. Don't care much about the mule, but it can haul that load for us awright, afore we feed it to our dogs."

"That was your last mistake," said Gideon.

"Which was?"

"Being so rude."

He drew both Colts before the highwaymen expected it or started to react. His first shot drilled Bert Wakefield just above his left eyebrow and cleared the saddle of his bay gelding. The second hit the man seated nearest on Bert's left a stunning blow to the sternum and pitched him over backwards from his dun mare, dead before he hit the dirt.

The other two were grabbing for their pistols then, more arrogant than handy with them. Thorn squeezed off his third and fourth shots almost simultaneously, dropping both of them, one spouting crimson from a punctured lung, the other clapping both hands to a frothing vent that opened up below his Adam's apple, cutting off his oxygen for good.

Only the lung-shot Wakefield had some life left in him by the time Thorn slid from Shadow's saddle to the road. His stallion wasn't gun-shy. Belle, in turn, seemed happy to be rid of the barbarians who'd threatened her.

The final Wakefield was beyond saving. He stopped breathing while Gideon replaced the four spent cartridges from his twin Colts, then thought about the problem that the highway ambush posed for him. He didn't like to meet the county's sheriff—Ethan Mallory, dead Bert had called him, tub of guts or otherwise—taking four corpses into his town before they had been introduced. Conversely, though, he couldn't simply act as if the killings hadn't happened.

What to do?

Thorn didn't take long to make up his mind. "I'm bound to share the news of this," he told his animals, "and I'll turn in what's easiest, their mounts included. As for Wakefields, I don't feel like hoisting them on board their mounts and having them leak all over those horses on the way to town."

The bandits' horses had begun to stray, but now Thorn called them back without moving his lips. They understood him right away and grouped around Shadow while Gideon stepped to their late masters, unbuckling each man's pistol belt and rolling deadweight off of them, draping one belt over each horse's saddle horn. That done, he drew their reins together, mounted Shadow once again, and led his new remuda westward toward Lake Village.

Half an hour later, as they entered town, pedestrians along the main street stopped and stared at Gideon. Thorn guessed he must've been a sight, a man dressed all in black, leading a mule and four riderless horses straight through town until he spied the sheriff's office on his left, adjacent to the Chicot County courthouse. Stopping there, while people gathered round at a respectful distance, whispering amongst themselves, Thorn took his time dismounting, tying Shadow's rains onto a hitching rail that stood beside a handy water trough, where Belle and Shadow both could quench their thirst.

Before he reached the wooden sidewalk, Ethan Mallory emerged from his office. Thorn didn't know him, but the brass star on his vest had SHERIFF stamped on it, to clear up any doubt concerning his identity.

Contrary to Bert Wakefield's harsh description, Mallory was slightly overweight, but not obese. As southern lawmen went, from what Thorn had observed while traveling, he was a trifle on the slim side for a sheriff—portly, if Thorn had to pin it down, but with a barrel chest and strong arms on him, legs in corduroy trousers that could've powered a much slimmer man. His face was on the square side, bushy brows and muttonchops beneath a roll-brimmed Stetson.

Eyeballing the crowd of townspeople before he spoke, the sheriff asked Thorn, "What's this all about, stranger?"

"Four men stopped me on the road," Gideon said, keeping it simple. "Said they planned to take my animals. I have no doubt they meant to kill me, in the bargain."

"And?"

"It didn't work out well for them."

"All dead?"

"And waiting for an undertaker, maybe two miles east of town. As you can see, I brought their guns and horses in."

"Who were these fellows?" Sheriff Mallory inquired.

"The talker called himself Bert Wakefield. Claimed the rest were relatives of his. Referred to one of them as Randy."

"I suppose the other two were Clint and Rowdy, then. Four brothers, not one of 'em worth a damn, and wanted over the half of Arkansas on sundry charges. Murder would've seen 'em hung. Some of the other counts were robbery and rape, barn-burning, rustling—well, you get the drift."

"So, you're not sad to see them go?" Thorn asked.

"The very opposite. In fact, between the four of 'em you're due a nice reward. Right around two thousand bucks, if I remember right. Payment's bound to take a little time, o' course."

"Can I just hand that over to your office, Sheriff? I'm no bounty hunter."

"Say again?"

"I didn't shoot them for a payoff," Thorn repeated. "I just didn't feel like giving up my animals, much less my life."

"Well, that beats all," Mallory said. "I'll have to sit down with Judge Kravitz, likely have you sign some kind of a release, but I imagine he can think of some deserving cause to take that kind of cash."

"I'll gladly sign off on whatever is required."

"That's mighty decent of you, Mr.—"

"Thorn. Gideon Thorn. I planned to come and see you on another, unrelated matter when the Wakefields tried to hold me up."

"Well, if you want to join me in my office, once I've sent somebody out to fetch them boys..."

"I'd like to get my animals placed at the livery before we talk, if that's all right with you. And maybe book a room at one of your hotels?"

"We've got two of 'em," Mallory replied. "The Grandee and the Chicot House. Both clean, well run. I'd be hard pressed to choose between 'em if I had to."

"Fine. I'll have a look around, then."

"Take your time, Sir. Counting the rewards and cost of trying them, you've likely saved the county six or seven thousand dollars as it is."

"I aim to please," Thorn said.

"And good aim, too, the way it stands."

"About that livery, Sheriff..."

"Oh, right. Go down to the south end of town and a block west off Main. Can't miss it."

"I'm obliged."

Thorn rode Shadow and led Belle to the livery, finding it exactly where the sheriff said that it should be. The hostler had an inch or two on Gideon, and thirty extra pounds, at least, his reddish beard apparent compensation for the fact that he was nearly bald. He introduced himself as Liam Coyle and seemed to be expecting Gideon, wringing his hand as if the two of them were long-lost friends.

"Half-price, Sir," Liam said, "as long as y'all may let me care for your fine animals."

Thorn smiled at Belle's reaction, something like a small voice saying, "Finally!" Having already noted reasonable rates posted outside, Gideon said, "I don't mind paying full rate for the days we're here."

"No, Sir. I'll not hear any more of that." Coyle dropped his loud voice to a confidential tone, adding, "Them Wakefields stole some horses offa me, a couple times, and used 'em something terrible. No good for anything from there on, were they. Had to put one of 'em down."

"Sorry to hear that," Thorn replied.

"Not your fault, Mr. Thorn. And now, you've put down *four* of them bastards!"

"Well..."

"I believe you'll find most folks around Lake Village view you kindly over that. I say 'most folks,' only because there's still a mess of Wakefields hidin' in the backwoods spread across Chicot and Ashley Counties. Ashley's over west of here."

"And they'll be mad about the others, I suppose?"

"No more 'n hornets in a hailstorm, I expect."

"All right, then. Good to know."

Gideon helped Coyle get his animals stabled, beaming out relaxing thoughts to help the stranger handle them first time. Before leaving, he paid three days at the half-rate Coyle still insisted on, then took his saddlebags, together with his two rifles, downtown to choose between Lake Village's hotels.

The Grandee and the Chicot House stood opposite each

other and a trifle catty-cornered on Main Street. Both bore fresh coats of paint and had a clean appearance, so he picked the one that was a half-block closer to him on the north side of the street.

When he walked into the Grandee, a clerk who looked as if he'd been in harness for a while—gray hair, eyebrows and mustache, in a pinstriped suit—offered effusive greetings before Thorn could say a word.

"Good afternoon, Sir! And may I say that it would be the Grandee's pleasure if you stayed with us while stopping over in Lake Village. After all you've done already—"

Gideon lifted a hand to stem the flow of words. "You win," he said. "I'm checking in."

"The first night complimentary, of course."

"This is a *really* friendly town," Thorn said, his mind adding, *So far*.

"Service is our profession, and in your case, a profound pleasure. Let's get you signed in right away, shall we? No other luggage, then?" One eyebrow rose a tick, then eased back down.

"I try to travel light," said Gideon, as he approached the desk and signed the Grandee's register.

"Well, if there's anything at all you may need, day or night, don't hesitate to ask, Sir. I'm Ralph Umbrage, manager. The night clerk will be Howard Janeway, also at your service."

"Excellent." Thorn took his key and went upstairs, moving along the second floor to reach a room that overlooked Main Street. He wouldn't have described it as luxurious, but it was clean and had all he would need in terms of furniture—chiefly a bed, a chifforobe, a washstand with a porcelain ewer, and one chair he would use to wedge the door shut when he was inside.

For now, he put his rifles in the chifforobe and left his saddle bags laid out across the bed's colorful comforter, then headed back downstairs and off to Sheriff Mallory's office.

The sheriff greeted him much as before, without the fervent handshake, telling Thorn, "Judge Kravitz reckons it'll be tomorrow before he can have the paperwork ready, if you're still wanting to unload the state's reward."

"I haven't changed my mind, and there's no rush," Gideon said. "I plan to be around another couple days, at least."

"More business in the neighborhood."

"Could be. I'm looking for a woman."

"Well, now, you can find 'em easy at one of our two saloons, the Busted Flush and Bayou Ben's."

Thorn smiled at that. "I didn't state my purpose clearly, Sheriff. I've come looking for a certain woman who, I'm told, dropped out of sight while she was looking into a peculiar local case with your newspaper editor."

"Ebb Gallatin? Puts out the *Lake Shore Sentinel,* you mean?"

"I didn't get a name," Thorn said, "but that's my information as of now."

"It's Ebb for Ebenezer. He's the paper's one-man show. And this 'peculiar' case..."

"I'm short on details, but I stopped in Little Rock while I was on my way down here from Arizona Territory. All I found in their daily reports was something about grave-robbing."

"Oh, right. *That.*" Mallory nearly spat the final word, as if it left a bad taste on his tongue. He wasn't looking cheerful anymore. "Not much that I can tell you about *that,* although o' course I looked into the crimes and all. As for some woman comin' in from outside, I don't know. Where did you say she hailed from?"

"Didn't say, and I'm not sure. Last time I saw her was about six months ago. We worked a job in Colorado, spent a little time in Kansas, then she went her way and I went mine. She gets around. A lady journalist."

"Hmm. I wish that I could tell you somethin', but o' course, feel free to visit Ebb, a couple blocks down at the *Sentinel*'s office."

Thorn checked his pocket watch and saw that it was getting on toward suppertime. "Maybe I'll catch him in the morning, Sheriff. Go and find something to eat just now. How many restaurants in town?"

"Three pretty good ones. Two—McCallister's and Johnson's—serve your basic fare. Bergeron's throws in some Cajun dishes that'll keep you warm all night, assuming that's a problem."

"Thanks again." Thorn hesitated. Asked, "Before I go, what can you tell me, generally about the grave robberies?"

"Well, they first started up around the tag-end of October, but the first ones passed unnoticed, cuz the body-snatchers, whatever you wanna call 'em, picked a back-woods cemetery nobody's been planted in since midway through the war. We've got a few or those around here. Families start buryin' their folks near home, then either die off later, or just up and move away."

"The bodies were removed and never seen again?"

"None of 'em's turned up yet, that I know of."

"So, taken, but not mutilated or abused in any other way that's provable?"

"Jesus! Who'd wanna do a crazy thing like that?"

"You'd be surprised at what some people do," Thorn said.

"Maybe before I put this badge on." Mallory reached up and tapped his chest. "Since then, well...I won't claim I've seen it all, but I've seen plenty."

Thorn hoped that he wouldn't have to see much worse but didn't want to bet on it.

"I don't suppose the opened graves focused on any certain family or groups that were related?"

"Not as I'm aware of. But you'll soon find out the people get tied up by marriage here in Arkansas—and all across the South, I guess—more so than folks in, say, Chicago or New York."

"Okay." Thorn's hand was on the doorknob when he thought of one more thing. "I've heard some talk around town that more Wakefields may be stopping by, looking for some way to avenge their kin."

"Lookin' for *you,* I guess you mean."

"It crossed my mind."

"Well, I don't know who told you that," said Mallory, "but whoever it was, I'd say they got it right. Wakefields are known for holdin' grudges and repayin' them in blood."

"No matter that they started it by trying to commit a felony?"

The sheriff rolled his shoulders in a shrug and nearly smiled at that. "It's what they do and have done, long as I've been knowin' them. I've seen more WANTED paper posted on that bunch than any other family that comes to mind, maybe since the James boys and Youngers. Payin' off the cash rewards on all of 'em would strain the state's budget, unless whoever put 'em down was nice and generous, like you."

"I'll keep my eyes peeled, just in case," Thorn said.

"A good idea for ever'body, not just them that's marked," said Mallory.

So now I'm marked twice, Thorn mused silently. *Once by the thing that massacred my family, now by the Wakefield clan.*

"Yes, Sir. Enjoyed the talk, Sheriff. If I hear anything about my missing friend, or I come up with any other questions..."

"Swing on by. Sure thing." Before Gideon could escape, Mallory asked, "About your friend. I didn't catch her name."

"And that was my mistake. It's Pilcher. Dinah Pilcher. If you want some background on her, send a telegram to the *Sagrado Sentinel* in San Diego, California. She used to run that paper. If it's still in business, whoever took over should have background information for you."

"Might do that. Meanwhile, try 'n enjoy your night here in Lake Village."

"That's the plan," Thorn said, and finally escaped.

From where he stood, all three of the town's restaurants were visible, but he was already leaning toward Bergeron's. Some spicy Cajun fare would suit him fine, and maybe help him stay alert tonight, if anybody came sniffing around with vengeance on his mind.

Gideon hoped it wouldn't come to that. He'd brought enough trouble to Lake Village already, but he wouldn't duck it, either.

Wait and see what happens, he decided, already alert as he paced off the sidewalk toward his chosen restaurant.

THREE

Thorn entered Bergeron's to find half of its twenty-odd tables already occupied. Unlike what he was used to in other small towns, most of the diners present smiled at him, as if in greeting, and the ones who didn't looked more quizzical than outright hostile. A brunette waitress led Gideon to a good table, facing onto Main Street, grinning at him fit to beat the band.

The grin slipped just a little when Thorn doffed his hat and let her see the white streak running down the central part in his black hair. She blinked once, then couldn't help asking, "Oh, Sir, does that hurt?"

"Not for a long time now."

She blushed a bit and hastily apologized. "Forgive me, please. I talk too much. Just seem to blurt out anything that comes to mind."

"It's not the worst trait I've encountered in my travels," Thorn replied.

She handed him a menu printed on cardboard, saying, "For you, o' course, the meals are free at Bergeron's."

"I really *can* afford to pay my way," he said.

"Not here, Sir. That's the word from Mr. Bergeron—Emile, his name is. Owns the place and does most of the cooking, too."

"Well..."

Stepping closer, lowering her voice, she said, "That lousy Bertram Wakefield and a couple of his kin got hold of Emile's niece one time, about two years ago. They hurt her bad, if you know what I mean." A deeper blush suffused her cheeks. "She lived but ran back home to Baton Rouge. Emile thought long and hard on killin' 'em himself but couldn't bring himself to take on the whole family, I guess. You made a friend for life with what you did today."

"All right. I thank him for his generosity," Thorn said, "and he's entirely welcome for the other."

"Please don't tell him that I mentioned it, will you? Like I told you,, I talk too much."

"Call it our secret."

"Perfect. My name's Karen, by the way. Karen Lee, but no relation to Robert from the war."

"I'm pleased to meet you, Karen Lee. Gideon Thorn."

"Oh, everyone in town knows that by now. Lake Village couldn't keep a secret if the whole town's life depended on it."

"I'll bear that in mind."

"So, have you tasted Cajun food before?"

"Just once."

That time had been at one of Boston's "specialty" cafés, the tactful way of saying Brahmins might not like it, but they ought to eat there anyway, to prove how cosmopolitan and open-minded they all were.

"Okay," Karen went on. "I like it all, myself, but keep in mind if anything says 'blackened,' that means extra-spicy, not just burnt up on the grill."

"That sounds familiar."

"I'll just let you look over the menu then. Something to drink?"

Thorn glanced around. "I know this isn't a saloon," he said. "But—"

"That's all right. Getting a drink around Lake Village is no problem any time but Sundays, when the blue laws say you can't have any fun. But even then, o' course, there's always shine around."

"I had some kind of beer in mind, if that's available."

"Yes, Sir! We carry what they put out from the Little Rock Brewery, also a couple brands from over to New Orleans. They've got a German, name of Merz, who makes a pretty good one, and two other breweries I can think of, Pelican and Lafayette. We've got 'em all."

"I'll try the Pelican, I guess."

"Good choice. Maybe you'll have a notion what you want for supper when I bring it back."

He did. Thorn started off with étouffée, a smothered seafood stew served over rice, and followed that with blackened catfish, plus a side order of "boudin balls" that proved to be pork sausage, rolled with green onions and rice, battered and fried. To cool it down, besides two mugs of Pelican, he got French bread with more than ample butter. Gideon managed to clean his plate but had to pass on Karen's offer of pecan pie for dessert.

He paid up when she wasn't looking, left two dollars more for Karen's service and the information she'd provided, then went out onto Main Street as dusk was creeping into Lake Village. A block east of the restaurant, Thorn saw light showing from the windows of the *Lake Shore Sentinel*'s office, and decided to drop in. There seemed no point in waiting till tomorrow morning, as he'd told the sheriff, if he had a chance to make some headway now.

Reaching the *Sentinel*'s doorway, Thorn tried the knob, found it unlocked, and pushed his way inside. A small bell overhead, attached to the doorframe, announced him and silenced the backroom clanking of what Gideon presumed must be a printing press.

"Coming right up!" a male voice called, before a figure cleared the intervening door. The man stood five foot six or seven, dressed to suit his calling in a vest and shirt with rolled-up sleeves, wearing a green eyeshade. His nimble-looking hands were stained with printer's ink, and he'd contrived to daub his chin with some, as well.

"Help you?" he asked.

"I'm hoping for a word with Mr. Gallatin."

"And here I am," the editor replied, showing his ink-blotched palms as he added, "Forgive me if I don't shake hands just now."

"That's fine."

"And you are—let me guess—Gideon Thorn, our hero of the hour?"

"Not exactly how I'd put it," Thorn replied. "But yes, I'm Thorn."

"You'll be the hero in tomorrow's *Sentinel,* I guarantee it. Not that most people in town don't know your story, as it is."

"Do they?" Thorn frowned.

"Of course! There's not a soul for fifty miles around who doesn't hold a grudge against the Wakefield tribe—except for other Wakefields, I suppose, but even some of them can't get along with one another."

"Folks keep telling me how ornery they are."

"And now you've seen it for yourself—making short work of them, from what I understand."

"That kind of work," Thorn said, "you take it slow, you likely won't come out of it in one piece."

"Spoken like a true shootist! May I quote you?"

"How's that?"

"Tomorrow's article," said Gallatin.

"That isn't why I'm here," said Gideon.

"Oh, no? What, then?"

"I understand you had a visitor some time ago. I couldn't say exactly when. Name's Dinah Pilcher. She's a journalist herself, and an old friend of mine."

"Dinah!" said Gallatin. "And what's she gotten up to since she left us?"

"Left you? Meaning..."

Gallatin was frowning now. "I mean we spoke about a story with some local interest—"

"The grave-robbing," said Thorn.

"Well, yes, in fact. You're well informed, I see."

"About Dinah..."

"I haven't seen or heard from her in nearly two weeks, now. We were supposed to meet again, compare notes as it were, but when I checked up on her at the Chicot House, she'd left with all her things. No forwarding address."

"You didn't find that any cause to be concerned?" asked Thorn.

"What, for her safety, do you mean? The truth be told—"

"I find that's always best," said Gideon.

"Of course. The fact is, she impressed me as a strong-willed woman, not unlikable, and easy on the eyes if I may say so, but..."

"But, what?" Gideon pressed.

"I didn't get a feeling that she'd found what she was looking for. When a reporter gets his teeth into a story—*hers,* in this case—there's no stopping them. They chase it to the end. I've told myself that she went seeking answers somewhere else and didn't hang around for any fond farewells."

"When you say seeking answers, that would be about your local case?"

"I'd guess so, but I couldn't swear to it. No other news came up around that time, as far as I've heard. She was definitely hoping to resolve our mystery—or, at the very least, report it to a wider reading audience."

"And she said nothing to suggest where she might go, if she got into a blind alley here?"

"Nothing. I would remember that, no doubt."

"All right." Thorn saw no point in playing his cards too close to the vest with Gallatin. "The story as I have it, from a friend I trust back east, is that she went missing—his word —while investigating a 'strange' case, his word again. Her being here, I take it that would mean your local corpse-snatching."

Gallatin nodded. "We've had nothing else to rival that since poor Josiah Stone went round the bend, killing his wife and little boy, nearly four years ago. That shocked us all, of course—a good church-going family and all—but would I call it strange?" The newsman shook his head, sadly. "Not in these troubled times."

"And I'd agree with you. Thing is, before I start to look for Dinah, I need to find out what leads, if any, she was chasing hereabouts. If you know anyone she might've interviewed, who might have any information on the crimes, or even just a vague suspicion...anything at all, right now, would be a help."

"Of course. I gave her two referrals, without thinking either one could tell her much of substance. Still, because the incidents involved graveyards, I said she might consult out local clergymen. I've personally pumped them dry, I think, but with a new slant and a comely face, who knows?"

Thorn tried to bring him back on point. "About those clergymen..."

"Yes, yes. Sorry! The only two we've got are Reverend Mayberry Hogan, with the Southern Baptist Church, and Father Malachi Glover, who serves the Catholics among us. As you might expect, they don't see eye-to-eye on most ecclesiastical matters, with Hogan being Protestant and Glover representing what Hogan refers to as the 'Whore of Babylon.' I swear, you put the two of them together and the sparks start flying. One time—"

"What about their views on the grave robberies"? Thorn interrupted him.

"Oddly, that's one point where they seemed to more or less find common ground, although their points of view are still divergent."

"Meaning what?" Gideon pressed.

"Simply that neither one believes a white man could perform such actions. No, they blame 'darkies,' as Glover phrases it—or 'niggers,' if it's Hogan talking. They suspect some taint of Voodoo creeping over from New Orleans, where there have been documented cases of bizarre activity, including claims of human sacrifice."

"But nothing to suggest that here? The sacrifice, I mean?"

"Well, no. But what would be the point?" asked Gallatin. "By definition, sacrifice requires a living man or animal, at least according to the Good Book. How could anybody hope to sacrifice a corpse? Why would they even try?"

"I hear you. As to bodies taken from the graves around here, can you say how many have been stolen?"

"I've tried keeping up with that, of course. I have a list of thirty-seven *white* corpses, which I believe is fairly accurate."

"You stress the white."

"I do. Alas, across our state and through the South at large, few whites regard Negroes as citizens. Some won't even admit they're human beings, if you can believe it. Until 1865, remember, it was criminal to educate a Negro, and no legal marriages were recognized amongst them, since it would've made selling their children off more problematic."

"And?"

"And any records of the Negro populace are spotty, incomplete at best. When one dies, there may be no death certificate on file. Burial in this climate can be hasty, simple markers don't last long—in short, unless someone is lynched or executed by the law, our county government may have no hard, fast evidence of who's alive or dead."

"And unless they're missed—"

"Which means missed by the other members of their race, unless they served in some capacity for white folks."

"They could disappear without a ripple," Thorn said.

"And I'd bet that any number of them have."

"Nobody's looking into that, I take it?"

"Anyone like whom? You mean the sheriff? Before he can begin investigating, someone has to claim a person's missing. The sheriffs in this state get all their votes from white men. With the colored folk, our Sheriff Mallory would likely think they'd just run off instead of fighting unfair labor contracts in the courts, with a white judge and jurors."

"Sounds like I need to visit Father Glover and Reverend Hogan."

"Couldn't hurt," said Gallatin. "Tomorrow is the fourteenth, I believe."

"Sounds right," Thorn granted.

"And it's Wednesday. Wednesdays around noon, you ought to find them playing checkers at the barbershop."

"Checkers? The way you spoke of them, that strikes me as peculiar," Gideon replied.

"For them to socialize?"

"I would've thought they'd fall to arguing their scriptures like you mentioned, maybe even come to blows."

"So, you're aware the Catholics read from a Bible that's unlike King James?"

"I've read them both," Thorn said. "Comparative religious studies, when I was at Harvard."

"That would certainly explain it. As to Wednesday checkers, let me say they're mainly enemies in church, on Sunday mornings and whatever other times they call their flocks together. Off the job, as you might say, they seem to get along all right. It's almost like they made a deal: no Bible-thumping during playtime. No homework at recess, as the kids in school might say."

"And it I happen on them playing checkers, what should I expect?" asked Thorn.

"Besides some irritation that you broke into their game? They will have heard of you by now. That's guaranteed. Whether they'll talk about the graveyard thefts, you being new to town and all, I couldn't say. That all depends on your approach, I'd guess."

"How would you win them over? As an outsider, I mean?"

"You have a leg up from your showdown with the Wakefields," Gallatin replied. "Beyond that, I can tell you Father Glover likes to pull a cork sometimes."

"And Hogan?"

"Being Baptist, he's teetotal. But he absolutely loves a good cigar."

"Okay, then. Is there anybody else you think I ought to see before I take a run at those two?"

With a shrug, Gallatin said, "If I could think of anyone who might know something, I'd have questioned them myself, by now. If somebody *does* have a handle on this thing, he's kept it strictly to himself, and that's not easy in Lake Village. I'd have said it was impossible, in fact, but what do I know? I moved here a bit before the war, and some old-timers still look on me like the new kid in a school."

"I know how that feels," Thorn said, thinking of his childhood days at Waverly Academy and in the Lawrence orphanage, before he'd learned to stand up for himself and not back down.

"It never goes away, does it?" asked Gallatin.

"Depends on how you face it," Thorn replied. "If you're intent on staying—"

"And I am," said Gallatin.

"Sometimes, if you can't change a person's mind, you have to let them be and wait for them to shuffle off the coil."

"A fatalist."

"Don't quote me," Gideon replied. "I move around so much, I'm pretty much the new boy anywhere I go."

"Aside from shooting outlaws if they brace you, what does that entail?"

"I work on jobs like this, where local law has given up or didn't care to start with. Sometimes, they just need a little push, to see a new way in. That doesn't mean they thank me afterward, mind you. So far, Lake Village strikes me as one of a kind."

"I'll take that as a compliment."

"It is." Thorn turned to leave, then stopped and asked, "You wouldn't know the padre's choice of poisons, would you?"

"Bourbon straight, or so I hear."

"I'm guessing I could find that and cigars at one of the saloons in town?"

"At either one of them," said Gallatin. "The Busted Flush or—"

"Bayou Ben's," Thorn finished for him. "Thanks. The sheriff clued me in on that."

"Drop into either one, I wouldn't be surprised if someone volunteers a round or three."

"Unless they're Wakefields, right?"

"Well, yes. Except for that. But I doubt they'll be coming into town this soon after...what happened on the highway."

"You doubt it, but you can't be sure."

Gallatin shook his head. "With Wakefields, no one can be sure of anything except they're mean and don't forget an insult or an injury, whether it's real or only in their minds."

"Sounds like you need a plague to wipe them out."

"From your lips, friend, to Someone's ear upstairs."

"I'm not sure we're on speaking terms," Thorn said, and closed the office door behind him as he left.

He chose the Busted Flush, since if was on his way back

to the Grandee. Bayou Ben's was farther down the street, a block past his hotel, which left a relatively quiet zone between the two saloons.

The place hadn't begun to hum when Gideon passed through its batwing doors, but there were ten to fifteen drinkers present, all of whom wanted to shake his hand before he'd reached the bar, some of them saying things like "Good job, Son" and "Way to give 'em hell."

The burly bartender was smiling through his gray-flecked Van Dyke beard as Gideon approached, asking, "What can I get for you? Your first shot's on the house—hey, make it two—or maybe you'd prefer to take a ride upstairs?"

Three soiled doves were descending polished stairs, all beaming at him, none of them exactly overdressed. Thorn smiled right back and told the barkeep, "I'm just passing through tonight. I need a fifth of bourbon, if that's possible, and how about a couple of your best cigars?"

"That's easy. Boss would skin me if I didn't charge you somethin' for the fifth, though. Can we call it half a dollar, and you'll get a quarter back if you return the bottle?"

"Eminently fair, my good man," Thorn replied, placing two dollars on the bar. "And buy the house a round, yourself included."

"Don't mind if I do, Sir."

He gave Thorn the whisky bottle and cigars in a brown paper bag, and there was more backslapping as Gideon left. Before he'd reached the street, the bar's piano player launched into a jangly version of "For He's a Jolly Good Fellow," with the patrons singing wildly out of key.

Some town, Gideon thought. *Some welcome.*

All he'd had to do was kill four strangers—and, presumably, whatever members of their twisted family came on behind them, looking for revenge. He'd lose no sleep over the shootings, but so far he'd come no closer yet to finding Dinah Pilcher.

And with every passing hour, Thorn could feel her slipping farther from his grasp.

FOUR

LAKE VILLAGE: MARCH 14, 1877

For breakfast, Thorn had tossed a mental coin and picked McCallister's over Johnson's, trusting the sheriff's word that both were restaurants of equal quality, guessing that Cajun fare twice in a row wouldn't turn out to be the wisest choice he'd ever made.

He missed Karen, her gift of gab, but waitress Molly at McCallister's turned out to be a cheerful redhead, pretty much as glad to meet him as Karen had been. Most of the early morning diners smiled or nodded at him, but Thorn guessed the glamour he'd acquired by killing four bandits would soon start wearing thin.

Breakfast—full charge, the cook apparently wasn't engaged in feuding with the Wakefields personally—was a Spanish omelet with a southern twist, including capers folded in the eggs with mushrooms, diced potatoes, onions, and parsley. The strips of bacon served beside it were sliced thick and wide, but grilled to perfect crispness, plus fresh biscuits dripping butter. When he'd finished every bite and downed a second cup of black coffee, Thorn paid and tipped, then took his leave, ambling along to reach the Western Union office that he'd spotted yesterday.

The clerk in uniform who greeted him by name, without an introduction, was somewhere in his mid-forties, deeply tanned, with a bland face and barrel chest. Thorn didn't reckon he was psychic, though, presuming that he'd heard of yesterday's exploit and either glimpsed Gideon on the street, or else absorbed some other townsperson's description of the new arrival.

He introduced himself as Henry, no last name, and asked Thorn, "Can I help you, Sir?"

"I need to send a wire to Boston."

"Absolutely. Yes, indeed." Henry supplied a blank form for the telegram, together with a stubby pencil that appeared to be the standard length wherever Thorn had dealt with Western Union in the past. He guessed they must start out full-size, but by the time he got around to them, they'd shrunken down.

He kept the message cryptic as he could, not worried about paying by the word, but more about whose eyes would scan it during transit. When he'd finished, it read:

> LAKE VILLAGE, ARK: THORN SENDS—SAFE ARRIVAL AND PURSUING CONTACTS. NO WORD YET CONCERNING OUR MUTUAL FRIEND. MORE SOON AS CIRCUMSTANCES WARRANT. G. T.

Henry counted the words, quoted a price, and Thorn settled the tab. Anxious to please, the clerk assured him, "I will get this on the wire directly, Sir."

"Appreciate it."

"Thanks for using Western Union. Stop in anytime!"

Thorn still had more than two hours to kill before surprising the two ministers over their game of barbershop checkers, so he decided on another visit to the sheriff's office. Ethan Mallory seemed glad enough to see him, but his features bore an overcast that Gideon interpreted as worry.

"Sorry to barge in," he said. "More trouble? I mean, if you're free to talk about it?"

"Well, it's trouble, all right—and it's not a secret—but I doubt that it connects to what you're working on, trying to find your lady friend."

"If there's a chance that talking through it could be helpful, I'm all ears."

"Okay," said Mallory. "I've got another body on my hands. One of the swamp folk brought 'im in—or what's left of 'im, anyway. Name's Asa Daughtrey. That's the stiff, not him as found it."

"So, he's local."

"Born and raised. Far as I know, the only time he spent outside of Chicot County was during the war. Hunter or poacher, call 'im what you will, he made his living killin' things, either for meat or sellin' parts of 'em, like hides 'n feathers, now and then a gator skull boiled down."

"What killed him?" Thorn inquired.

"That's where I run into the problem. Last time anybody will admit to seein' him alive was four, five days ago. Said he was goin' after gators on Lake Boggy Bayou, and that's where his corpse was found. His skiff, too, with a rifle in it, though *he* wasn't in the boat."

"I see the problem."

"Sure, you do. Four days and nights, or maybe five, lyin' in mucky water full of fish and turtles, snakes 'n gators, crabs and who knows what-all, that'll make a damn mess out of anybody. But the thing is..."

Thorn waited, then pressed him. "What?"

"Even the way that he was swollen up, discolored like a floater gets, and after anything that came along got tired of snacking on 'im, markings on his neck still make me wonder whether someone mighta choked the life out of 'im first, before they tossed 'im in the drink."

"Known enemies?" Thorn asked.

"With swamp folk, who 'n hell knows? Some of his hunting may've been against the law, not that the rules have ever really been enforced. Still, no one I can think of woulda tried to strangle him with Asa packing that .58-caliber rifle or his six-gun from the war. He emptied both of 'em before he died, in case I didn't mention that."

"That *is* a problem."

"Not yours, anyway...unless you wanna come along and take a look at 'im. I'm heading for the undertaker's now. Share your professional opinion, if you would."

"I'm not sure that applies to this, but why not? I've got time before I try to catch your local clergy at their Wednesday checker game."

Leaving the office, Mallory said, "Sounds like something yon Ebenezer would suggest."

"Ah. Yes, he did, in fact."

"I guess he couldn't help you trace your friend, himself?"

"He definitely met with her and shared some information on the cemetery robberies. They were supposed to meet again—or so he thought—when she cleared out of her hotel with all her things, no forwarding address. Unless somebody else has heard from her since then, I'm stumped."

"She had words with the preachers, though?"

"That's Gallatin's impression, but he wasn't with her, if she did, and never got a chance to hear about it afterward."

"Damnation. That must be as frustratin' as all get-out."

"I'd say."

"Well, here we are at Roscoe Cagle's. He's the undertaker. Likes to joke about it, sayin' he's the last man who will ever let you down. Gives me the creeps, sometimes."

They entered the mortician's parlor and were met by the proprietor. At first glance, Roscoe Cagle had a frail appearance, but Gideon felt the strength in his handshake and guessed the years of lifting corpses, toting caskets, had to put some muscle on his slender frame, concealed by somber suits that went with undertaking.

"Mr. Thorn," said Cagle, with a narrow smile. "Your reputation goes before you, Sir. And thank you for the extra business."

"Any Wakefields comin' in to fetch their kin?" asked Sheriff Mallory.

"No word from out their way as yet. Of course, if I knew where they were, exactly, you could round them up and clear some warrants, eh?"

"If I could find somebody for a posse to go hunting them."

"So, maybe not. Shall I alert you, Sheriff, if and when they happen by?"

"Only if you can do it without any peril to yourself or Mrs. Cagle."

"Bearing that in mind, of course."

"Well, anyhow, we've come to take another look at Asa Daughtrey. First look for my friend here, as you know."

"Of course. No family to raise any objections that I

know of. And it *is*, as you'd agree, something of a suspicious death."

"You told that straight."

"This way, then, gentlemen."

They trailed Cagle into his workshop, set behind his business office and what some morticians liked to call a "slumber room," where the departed were briefly displayed for family and friends, before their final journey to a church —if they were so inclined—then on to the graveyard.

A body covered by a sheet was laid out on Cagle's work-table, and he drew the shroud back to present a clear view of the corpse from head to feet. Gideon saw at once what Mallory had meant about the body being water-logged, both somewhat bloated and discolored from submersion, various chunks missing from the torso and extremities, together with a gaping bite wound on Asa's left cheek, exposing what teeth he'd possessed and part of his jawbone.

"Now, here," said Mallory, pointing, "if you look close enough, around his neck, you'll see what I was tellin' you."

Thorn leaned in, held his breath, and saw it plain enough: apparent bruises that resembled finger marks on each side of the dead man's throat, as if someone had grabbed and choked him from behind. Straightening up and stepping back a pace, he said, "It's there, all right. If someone didn't try to strangle him, whether it did the job or not, I don't know what else would leave marks like that."

"So, murder, then."

"I'd say, whether the strangulation finished him, or he was left to drown. Killing was the intent. As to his cheek..."

"A bite mark," Mallory declared. "I couldn't say what did it, though."

"Does it look roughly man-sized to the two of you?" Thorn asked.

"Well..."

"Lord have mercy!" Cagle said. "Now that you mention it, it *does*."

"You think a *man* bit off part of his face?" asked Mallory.

"I won't say that, but in a fierce fight," Gideon replied, "I've seen ears torn away, and even once, part of a nose."

"It's definitely not unheard-of," Cagle said.

"Well, shit. That's all I need right now, on top of ever'thing."

"Sorry," Gideon said. "Wish I could tell you something more, but I'd be guessing blindly."

"Sure. I understand," the sheriff said. "Well, Roscoe, thanks for showin' us. I'll see if I can get Tom Howard to come over with his camera, for all the good that it'll do. Maybe preserve some kinda crazy evidence at least, so you can go ahead and get him in the ground."

"I hate to mention it, Sheriff," the undertaker said.

"Oh, right. If no one claims him, I suppose the county has to pay, but keep it on the cheap. A plain pine box and no marker, if nobody's likely to come around and look for 'im."

"I understand, of course."

Thinking of the bite mark on the victim's face, Thorn couldn't help remembering the job he'd just wrapped up in Arizona Territory. There'd been no trace of humanity about the creatures he'd faced there, but they had been the deadly products of a "brilliant" mind, which told him damned near nothing was impossible.

Glad to be out of Cagle's place, and still with time to spare before his unexpected drop-in at the barbershop, Thorn happily agreed when Sheriff Mallory proposed seeing Judge Kravitz to resolve the pending paperwork on the Wakefield rewards.

The Chicot County courthouse, as he'd noted on arrival, was the centerpiece of Main Street, although less impressive to the eye than most Yankees might well expect of southern law and order. It had managed to survive the war without apparent damage, but its brick façade was something of a letdown, if you came expecting white imported marble. It had four Corinthian columns in front, flanking its plain gray concrete steps, but they'd been carved from wood and painted white, skipping expensive stone. The paint had started flaking now, and if someone had been assigned to upkeep, he was definitely slacking off.

Inside, the lobby floor was tiled, with offices to each side and a courtroom straight ahead, in back. Another pair of smaller courtrooms filled the second floor, on either side of a broad staircase carpeted in Tartan plaid that ran to navy blue with gold cross-hatching.

"Scottish architects?" asked Thorn.

"From what I understand, somebody got it on the cheap," said Mallory. "The judge's chambers are this way."

Thorn followed his guide to the left of the staircase, where Mallory rapped on a tall, dark wooden door. Inside, a deep voice called out, "Enter!" and they did.

Judge Kravitz, for a start, looking nothing like Thorn had expected from his voice. He was a small man, not quite wizened, pushing seventy at least. Gideon half-expected him to have a black robe on, but he was dressed in a gray linen suit over a white shirt, with a red bowtie. His balding head seemed too large for his body, and he peered through spectacles that had no metal frame, the earpieces attached to the lenses on either side. Whenever he saw glasses of that type, Gideon thought they must be devilish to repair.

"The celebrated Mr. Thorn!" said Kravitz, stepping forward with his hand extended. Thorn shook it, pleased to discover that the judge's grip was neither soft nor clammy.

"I don't know about the 'celebrated' part, Your Honor," he replied.

"You're celebrated here," said Kravitz, "though I grant that doesn't count for much."

"You have a friendly town," Gideon said, smiling.

"Except for Wakefields, eh?"

"I didn't plan—"

"Tut-tut! You're in the clear, Sir. In some ways—*most* ways, I'd guess—we're still what most would call a frontier town. No matter that the county was established better than one hundred fifty years ago. Rumors claim Hernando de Soto lies somewhere under Lake Chicot, but how his soldiers could have dug the grave escapes me. Others claim he never made it this far north, but died around eight hundred twenty miles due south, along the Mississippi, in Concordia Parish, Louisiana."

"What are your thoughts?" Thorn inquired.

"Try not to think about it, personally," Kravitz answered. "Dead Spaniards don't mean a lot to me. Well, on to business, eh?"

The paperwork was simple, Kravitz telling Thorn that when he signed, he'd be surrendering any and all claims to the Wakefield rewards that totaled $2,100. Thorn said that was fine with him and inked his name along the line labeled "WAIVING PARTY," while Judge Kravitz and the sheriff signed as witnesses. Last thing, the judge produced an iron embosser from a lower desk drawer and impressed the faux vellum with Chicot County's seal, beside their signatures.

"All done, Sir, and the county thanks you," Kravitz said. "We'll find some way to make that money work for us."

"Suits me," Thorn reaffirmed.

"I understand you've cast your eye upon our difficulty with the midnight ghouls."

"Mainly, I'm looking for a friend last seen while staying here in town, to write about the crimes."

"The lady journalist. Don't look surprised," Judge Kravitz chided him. "I heard that from the sheriff, here, but it could just as well have been the street sweeper. If you break wind around Lake Village, everyone in town knows what you had for lunch. We're not much on preserving secrets, I'm afraid."

"I'm not sure I'd agree with that, Your Honor," Thorn replied. "Aside from my friend disappearing—if she did—you've had somebody robbing graves for months, and now you've got what looks like murder on your hands."

"Asa?" Kravitz turned his gaze on the sheriff, chin tucked down to peer over his spectacles. "I thought he drowned, Evan."

Mallory shook he head. "Looks now like he was strangled before someone left 'im floating in the slough."

"Well, dammit! That needs looking into, Sheriff."

"First thing on my list, Judge, you can rest assured."

"Old men don't rest that easily, particularly with the weight of a whole county on their shoulders. People will expect a trial, if it was murder. They'll expect a hanging."

"I'd kinda like to find the killer first, Judge. Now, if you don't mind..."

Back on Main Street, Thorn checked his watch and saw that it was nearly noon. He parted company with Sheriff Mallory and stopped at the Grandee—another fulsome greeting from the manager—and fetched the offerings of liquor and tobacco from his room. It felt strange, carrying those tokens of venial sin to a chat with two preachers, but Thorn didn't mind a little bribery if it produced results.

The barbershop was small-town standard, a man of middle years seated in its lone chair, getting a shave. Left of the doorway, at a table by the shop's window, two men in black suits, both wearing clerical collars, peered at one another with a checkerboard between them.

"Won't be long, Sir," said the barber.

"Maybe later," Thorn replied. "I'm here on other business at the moment."

By the time he reached the table, both men had their eyes on Gideon—not hostile, but reserved, waiting for Thorn to state his business.

"Gentlemen," he said, "I'm—"

"We know who you are," the gray-haired cleric to his left declared.

"Fellow who shot the Wakefields," his companion—slightly younger, with a bald spot at his crown—added.

"Guilty as charged," Thorn said.

"There's no crime in an act of self-defense," said Gray Hair.

His partner quoted Genesis, saying, "Whoso sheddeth man's blood, by man shall his blood be shed: for in the image of God made he man."

"Well, thank you. Sheriff Mallory suggested I should talk to both of you about the graveyard incidents that have been going on around your county for a while."

The ministers exchanged a long and silent glance, then Gray Hair flicked his eyes off toward the barber, lowering his voice to say, "Someplace more private, like the street, perhaps."

Thorn stepped back, saying, "At your pleasure."

"We'll come back and finish later, Jimmy," said the younger minister, as both men rose and led the way outside. When they were outside, out of earshot, Gray Hair introduced himself as Reverend Mayberry Hogan, his companion as Father Malachi Glover. That done, hands shaken all around, the priest asked, "How did Evan think that we could help you, Mr. Thorn?"

"Please, make it 'Gideon'."

"The trumpeter of God," said Hogan.

"Also called Jerubbaal," Glover chimed in.

"Nobody's ever called me that before," Thorn said.

"About these robberies of graves," Hogan began.

"First thing," Thorn interrupted him, "the sheriff doesn't think that either one of you had any part in what's gone on."

"That should go without saying," Glover huffed.

"And we'll pretend it did, shall we?" Hogan added.

"Of course, and my apologies," said Thorn. "His gist was that you might be able to enlighten me about the *kind* of people who might do such things. But first—"

He pulled the fifth of bourbon and cigars from pockets of his coat, passing them to Hogan and Glover. The padre quickly tucked his bottle out of sight, eyeing the street for witnesses, while Hogan fired up a cigar, the other disappearing into his breast pocket.

"We'll walk and talk," said Glover, not asking a question. Flanking Thorn, they moved on down the wooden sidewalk, stopping in mid-sentence if they met other townspeople on the way.

"My guess would be Voodoo," said Hogan. "Might you be familiar with it, Gideon?"

"I've done some reading up on it," Thorn said, avoiding

reference to all the other outré subjects he had studied diligently over time.

"Down here, my son, we *live* with it. The colored folk...well, I supposed it's not their fault, exactly, coming over from their homeland as they did, in chains, compelled to hear the gospel from their captors when they weren't allowed to read the Bible for themselves."

"I'll have to disagree with you on that, Malachi," Hogan interrupted. "Slavery as found in the United States may not have been ideal, but it *is* sanctioned in the Bible. And without it, how would all those poor, lost souls ever have come to Jesus Christ?"

Glover addressed himself to Thorn, saying, "Forgive Mayberry, Gideon. He is a *Southern* Baptist, after all. As you may know, they left the parent church in 1845, to take the side of slaveholders."

"Is it my fault that nigras bear the mark of Cain, destined for servitude from Genesis on down? And what of Exodus 21, Malachi? 'And if the servant shall plainly say, I love my master, my wife, and my children; I will not go out free—"

"Mayberry—"

But the other minister talked over him, still quoting: " 'Then his master shall bring him unto the judges; he shall also bring him to the door, or unto the door post; and his master shall bore his ear through with an awl; and he shall serve him forever.' "

"That was ancient Canaan, Mayberry, as you know very well!"

"Gentlemen, please," said Gideon. "We've gotten off the point. Voodoo, remember?"

"Hmpf!" Hogan grunted. "If its *Voodoo* you're after, I can only think of one person who knows it inside-out."

"Erasmus Jones," said Glover.

Hogan nodded solemnly. "The very same."

"And where might I find Mr. Jones?" Thorn asked.

"I don't know any *Mister* Jones," Hogan replied. "But if you seek the *nigra* Jones, you'll find him in the freedmen's quarter, east of town. Where else?"

FIVE

Thorn stopped at Johnson's restaurant for lunch, returning nods and cautious smiles to the assembled diners who acknowledged him, letting the others slide. It still took him aback to face something besides suspicion in a town confronting dark deeds after nightfall, but on balance it made a refreshing change.

The waitress here was brunette and pretty, on the young side, without seeming shy. She briefed him on the daily specials and he went for pot roast with a mix of vegetables, together with a baked potato on the side that could've been a meal all by itself. Like Bergeron's, Johnson's had beer on tap and Thorn ordered a mug to go with lunch, already thinking that another might not hurt if he was going to be chatting later with a Voodoo priest.

During his studies of comparative religion, both at Harvard and under his Aunt Drusilla's roof, Thorn had acquired a superficial working knowledge of the supernatural beliefs some Africans had practiced in their homeland and continued after coming to America in chains. In fact, it went by sundry variations of that name: *Vodun* across West

Africa, where many slaves began their miserable transit to the New World; *Vodum* in Brazil; *Vodú* in Cuba; *Vudú* or "21 Divisions" on Santo Domingo; and *Vodou* in neighboring Haiti. *Voodoo* was mostly heard throughout Louisiana and environs, but the varied spellings didn't have much impact on its rituals.

As slaves dispersed, so their native religion was adapted and concealed from their white masters, mostly staying undercover since the Civil War. A major branch of *Vodum* in Brazil was called *Candomblé*, translated from Portuguese as "dance in honor of the gods." Elsewhere, in the United States and farther south, you might run into *Santería*, whose adherents also worshipped—or disguised their pagan gods—behind the guise of Catholic saints. *Obeah*, geared chiefly toward ritual healing, was also found throughout the West Indies. *Palo* Mayombe—"stick magic" was rooted in the Congo, named for use of sticks, or sometimes bones, to stir the contents of a caldron dubbed *nganga*, either seeking to divine the future or appease the nine old gods collectively known as *orishas*.

Thorn could see the draw of sects brought over from the African homeland, mixed up in varied ways with Christianity white owners forced upon their bondsmen, preaching to them from a Bible they were not allowed to read or study for themselves. Why not conceal the tenets of your faith in times when slaves were barred from education, even legal marriage, sweating out their days under the lash in cotton fields or serving in their masters' homes, where child abuse and rape of women were routine?

Thorn's meal arrived, and he enjoyed it thoroughly, taking a second beer when he was halfway done. His mind, meanwhile, was far away and back in time, before Emancipation and the Reconstruction era that had seen freedmen returned to something very much like antebellum slavery under the guns of white lawmen and vigilantes from the Ku Klux Klan. That secondary civil war had been played out across Dixie and in the Border South, where slave states "loyal" to the Union showed remarkable, brutal resistance to the final liberation of their black captives.

The first state readmitted to the Union had been Tennessee, in 1866. Six more of the late rebel states were reunited with America in June of 1868, then passed draconian "Black Codes" expelling blacks from politics, returning them to lowly servitude and prompting Congress to establish military occupation districts where the U.S. Constitution would—at least in theory—be enforced with bayonets. White vigilantes ran amok at that, leading to passage of the Ku Klux Act and imposition of martial law in certain Klan-infested counties, jailing some white terrorists while most escaped.

In Arkansas, a so-called "Black Militia"—always led by whites, even where some of the recruits were freedmen—helped to crush the KKK and stifle bloody feuds between some of the Razorback State's backwoods families. Unless Thorn missed his guess, the local Wakefields had escaped that purge of bandits and hung on in far southeastern Arkansas because most of the state's top men hoped they would finally die off and disappear.

Glad I could help with that, Gideon thought, while ordering a slice of apple pie for his dessert.

When he was done and took his leave of Johnson's, Thorn decided on another visit to the *Lake Shore Sentinel*'s office and Ebenezer Gallatin.

The problem, as Thorn understood the white resistance to Voodoo, was twofold. First, any religion that was mostly black, especially with ties to Africa, sparked fears of revolution like the one in Haiti that had climaxed in 1804. The second was a matter of involvement in both animal and human sacrifice, although the latter was supposed to be a rarity. The Holy Bible was replete with sacrifices of all kinds, demanded by the "one true God," but when the marching orders came from someone else...well, that set many white folks foaming at the mouth and tying hangman's knots.

When Thorn entered the *Sentinel*'s office, Gallatin was at the front desk, signing up an advertiser. Gideon gave them some space, examining the paper's tear sheets pinned up on one wall, and nodded as the customer departed, touching his hat brim in greeting as he left.

"Ah. Mr. Thorn," said Gallatin. "You're back."

"Looks like.'

"And how may I help you today?"

"I followed your advice and caught the clergy playing checkers. You were right about their taste in bribes—so, thanks for that—and also on their views of Voodoo."

"I thought so. And your take on what they said?"

"They both agreed I ought to see a colored follow called Erasmus Jones, residing somewhere east of town in what they called the freedmen's quarter."

"I know Jones," said Gallatin, glancing around the office as he spoke. It almost seemed to Thorn as if he thought someone might be concealed there, eavesdropping, although there was nowhere for them to hide.

"And have you spoken to him?"

"No, no," Gallatin responded with a headshake. "This may strike you oddly, coming from the East, but down here, things are...different."

"I gathered that. Still, with a story like this going on..."

"How can I put this delicately? I don't have any colored

subscribers, and the whites who take the *Sentinel* don't like to think about our racial problems. Rather, I should say, they think about them all the time, but don't appreciate having the dirty laundry aired in public, if you take my meaning."

"No stories about the Negroes, then," Thorn said.

"Oh, I can write about them to my heart's content, if they're being arrested, maybe killing one another on the odd occasion. That's *expected,* don't you see? A story that comes over sounding positive about them...well, I either let that go or use a name without referring to the subject's race."

"And if somebody's harming them?"

"I'd notify the sheriff, but my readers wouldn't want to be involved with that."

"Uh-huh."

"I understand your disappointment, Sir."

"Don't let it trouble you. How would I find this Mr. Jones?"

"Erasmus? As the preachers said, he's over in the freedmen's quarter."

"East of town," said Thorn, "but that covers a lot of territory."

"It's *immediately* east," said Gallatin. "If we had railroad tracks running through town, I'm fairly certain that would be the 'wrong' side."

"No specific address?"

"Not where you're going. Just ask anyone. They all know where he lives, but whether they'll direct a white man there...well, that's another matter altogether."

"So, just take my chances, then?"

"Another time, I'd take you out myself, but since the *Sentinel*'s a weekly paper, coming out tomorrow..."

"Right. I'd rather keep this private for the moment, anyway," Thorn said. "But thanks."

Outside, he started toward the livery, then noticed two disreputable-looking men across the street, standing beside a pair of horses at a hitching rail. They watched Thorn pass, not saying anything or making any gestures to him, but their faces instantly reminded Gideon of four dead Wakefields lying over at the undertaker's parlor. Not exact, mind you, but close enough to pass for kin.

Gideon thought about reversing his direction and reporting his observers to the sheriff, but aside from a gut feeling, he had nothing else to base an accusation on. And if they *were* Wakefields, what could Ethan Mallory do legally to run them off? Unless he had their faces on his WANTED posters, coming into town wasn't a crime.

And say he ran them off, then what? They could ride home, collect more vengeful relatives, and come back after dark.

Thorn ducked into the Grandee long enough to fetch his Winchester and came out with it in his left hand, making sure the watchers knew he was well armed before he moved on to the livery. He helped the hostler saddle Shadow, spent a moment telling Belle good-bye for now, then rode off to the east, seeking wrong side of a nonexistent railroad line.

Thorn had no problem telling when he reached the freedmen's quarter. There, the homes were mostly rundown shacks made out of scrap lumber and tarpaper. The roofs were either rusty tin or thin plywood, some of the latter with more tarpaper spread over them. There were no gutters on the eaves, just muddy ruts where rain ran off and gouged the ground. A fair share of the roofs had grass or weeds sprouting on top of them.

The quarter's people lined its rutted street to watch him pass, some looking fearful, others with defiance in their eyes. Whereas the white folks of Lake Village seemed to like Thorn more or less, to coloreds he was just another paleface bearing guns, potential danger on the hoof.

Thorn dreaded asking any of them for directions to Erasmus Jones, but as it turned out, the inquiry wasn't necessary after all. The biggest house in town stood on its own, as far back as the road could take him before disappearing into trees, and someone had maintained it better than the other shacks Gideon had observed. It had a covered porch, with wind chimes decorating it and clanking softly in the breeze.

Thorn almost reached the house before he realized the chimes were bleached-out bones, most of them readily identified as barnyard fowl or those of small mammals. A few, however, made Thorn frown and wonder how Jones came by them.

Stature aside, the house he'd pegged as Jones's stood apart from its neighbors by fifty feet or so and was constructed out of normal planks, versus the scraps employed by other builders in the freedmen's quarter. It was also freshly painted, sometime in the past year pr two Thorn guessed, while other hovels in the quarter were bare wood, much of it warped, with two or three whitewashed so long ago the lime and water mixture used had faded over time. The Jones house—if it *was* his—was predominantly black, with every fourth plank painted red, a color scheme inviting speculation on the goings-on inside.

It also had a hitching post out front, suggesting mounted visitors from town or farther off. The only animals that Thorn had seen around the quarter so far were two stray dogs with their ribs showing and one swaybacked, unhappy looking mule.

Gideon reined Shadow to a halt before the house, dismounted, and left him with calming thoughts, instead of being tethered where he stood. If anything went badly wrong from here on out, at least the stallion could escape.

Thorn stepped up to the porch, confirming that the nearest wind chime was made out of something's ribs, and knocked on the front door. It opened almost instantly, as if the occupant had seen him coming and was waiting for him to arrive.

"Mr. Erasmus Jones?" he asked.

"Mister. I see you don't come from around here, then."

"No, I—"

"You sound like Massachusetts, Mr. Thorn."

"Have we been introduced?" Gideon asked.

"No need for that, is there?" Stepping back, Jones cleared the doorway, adding, "May as well come in here, then, and see if I can satisfy you."

Once the door was shut again, two lamps and sunshine streaming through thin curtains lit the house inside. Its living room and kitchen were combined, with two more doors leading to rooms in back. The walls were decorated with more bones, bunches of feathers, and several snake skins: Thorn picked out an eastern diamondback, two copperheads, and one with colored rings that might have been a coral snake. The shotgun standing upright in a corner had a well-oiled look about it.

"I am not what you expected, eh?" said Jones.

"I had no preconception." Gideon replied, although that wasn't strictly true. He'd pictured in his mind a man shorter than Jones's six foot two or three, leaner than his 180 pounds or so. As far as age, his host defied guesswork:

gray hair turning to white around the temples, deep lines on his face that could've come from decades spent on Earth, hard work under the sun,

"Well, that's a first. You'd be a most peculiar white man then, considering what you came here to talk about."

"Which is?"

"What else? Grave robberies, o' course, and we should not forget about your missing friend."

It was too soon for Thorn to take that bait. Instead, he asked, "Did someone tell you to expect me, Mr. Jones?"

"Some *thing* is closer to the fact. I scried you, Mr. Thorn, without knowing your name at first, o' course. That would've been when you were crossing Texas, closing in."

"You're saying it was magic?" Gideon inquired.

"Magic, the second sight, *orishas* talking in my head. It's all the same to me."

"Let's say that I believe that..."

"You've seen stranger things before, I think, and plenty of 'em, going back to when you were a child."

"That's interesting," Thorn said, thinking that it could've come from listening to recent gossip around town.

"Lake Village people don't come out here much," Jones said, as if responding to Thorn's silent thought. "A few, o' course, for little remedies and potions, but they keep it quiet from the others and they don't stay on to socialize."

"The color line?"

"Is wide and bright," said Jones. "You crossed it at the edge of town back there a bit."

"I gathered that from—"

"Their two ministers, so called? To each his own, but I wouldn't trust either one of them with my immortal soul. Still, we owe you a favor, out here in the Quarter."

"Oh?"

"For killing Wakefields. They've been making trouble for us since the war—and long before it, too."

"They forced that on me," Thorn replied.

"And so, your hands are clean. Now, as to business."

"The grave robberies," Thorn tried again.

"I don't need second sight to know the church men think I must've been behind it. I expect a lynching mob some night, you know. It wouldn't be the first time."

"If I find out who's behind these crimes, it could defuse that situation."

"For a little while, perhaps. There's always some excuse to kill a colored man or two."

Thorn nodded. "Will you help me, anyway?"

Jones smiled. "First, you want to discover if any of *our* graves have been disturbed."

"I'm told the sheriff wouldn't know if they had been, or not."

Jones shrugged. "We bury some, burn others. It depends on what the person lost to us believed in life, if anything."

"I'll take that as a 'no,' as to the thefts from graves."

"Some of our folk, however, disappear from time to time, while they are still alive. The swamps, you know...or something else."

"I'd be surprised if you don't have a thought regarding that," Thorn said.

"You've made a study of Voodoo? Yes, I can see you have."

"In school, a bit." Thorn didn't mention Harvard, saw no point in showing off.

"And well before that too, I think. Your...aunt, was it?...sampled religions of all sorts. You do the same."

Thorn tried to keep his face deadpan while sorting

through his thoughts. There was no way he could divine that anyone around Lake Village might know anything about his childhood or his Aunt Drusilla in Boston.

Jones nodded, satisfied with Gideon's silent reaction. "Have you heard of zombies, eh?"

"The living dead raised from their graves by magic."

"Ah. But there are *two* kinds. One sort is alive, in fact, as you or I, breathing, seeing, hearing, but they have lost the power to control their minds."

"How's that work?"

"There are potions," Jones replied, "and poisons, some derived from plants, others from certain fish, or even toads. If introduced correctly, they present an image indicating death and may result in funerals before one is required. Whether the victims seem to die or not, they lose control over their will and must obey the orders of the first person who wakes them from their sleep."

"And what's the point of that?" Thorn asked.

"Sometimes, to punish enemies by forcing them to act as they would not have done in life. They may attack a relative or close friend in their trance state, to repay old or imaginary wrongs against their maker. Also, they may serve their masters as the slaves of old, demanding only meager sustenance and no care beyond that." Another shrug before he said, "And if they die, in fact...well, who would be surprised?"

"You said two kinds of zombies," Thorn reminded him.

"The other, as you said before, are corpses brought to life. They may be weakened by decay, but while they last, they also follow orders from their masters: killing, working, simply wandering about to cause disorder in the neighborhood."

"But if they're truly dead—"

"How may their souls be laid to rest?" Jones always seemed to be one step ahead of Thorn. "There are no antidotes, as with the poisons that I mentioned earlier, but there are conjurations, spells and such that may prove helpful."

"May?"

"Some undead zombies, if too much time passes after resurrection, drift beyond the physical control of those who raised them. As you might suspect, their brains and minds decay along with muscle, flesh, and bone."

"And when that happens...?"

"It is unpredictable, I fear. Some drop dead where they stand and cannot rise again, regardless of the invocations used upon them. Others...well, I've heard of some—not seen it for myself, you understand—who use their dying strength to go on missions of their own design."

"Can't say I like the sound of that," Thorn said.

"Nor should you. Nor should anyone. A zombie with no master in control would be...*une chose terrible*."

"You speak French, as well," Thorn said.

"And you?"

"*Assez pour comprendre*," Thorn said, meaning enough to understand the spoken word.

"It's very common in Louisiana," Jones said. "*Y también hay mucho español*."

Gideon smiled at that, and said, "You'd take some of your neighbors by surprise."

"White men are not my neighbors, Mr. Thorn, although we occupy the same space on our planet for the time being."

"A white ago," Gideon said, "you asked about my missing friend. Do you know anything about her?"

"I know she was curious," Jones answered, "but she did

not come to see me. Possibly she would have, if there had been time."

"Are you saying she's dead?"

"That, I confess, is closed to me," Jones said. "I wish that I could help you, but it lies beyond me. I cannot lift that veil."

"Mind if I ask why not?"

"Someone...some *thing*...prevents it. There is power working here, perhaps beyond my capabilities. I'm truly sorry. You must seek her on your own."

"That's what I'll do, then," Thorn said, turning toward the door. "Thanks for your time and help."

"Such as it was, eh? Possibly, I raise more questions than I answer."

"That can be a help, all by itself."

"I wish you luck. If you have need to call on me again...feel free."

"Obliged."

Thorn left that strange house, mounted Shadow, was nearly back in town before the Wakefields crossed his mind again.

SIX

LAKE VILLAGE

Sheriff Ethan Mallory knew trouble when he saw it, and in Chicot County, its primary name was "Wakefield." Spotting two of them on Main Street in broad daylight, early afternoon, he detoured by his office and paged through his WANTED posters, searching for their faces, but despite a striking family resemblance, it appeared that neither one of them was being actively pursued just now.

Too bad.

Hedging his bets, he peered out through his office window, making sure they hadn't bolted after seeing him, then loosed his holster's hammer thong and took a double-barreled twelve-gauge from the gunrack as backup. Stepping outside again, he made a beeline for his targets, cutting cattycorner across Main and watching them watch him approach, careful to keep their hands clear of the pistols on their hips.

"John Law!" the older of them greeted Mallory as he

drew near. "You reckon we've disturbed the peace, just standin' here?"

"Disturbed the peace," his kinsman echoed, sounding like an idiot who'd never had a whole thought of his own.

"If I thought that," said Mallory, "I'd likely open up the two of you and show the townsfolk what you had for breakfast."

"Sounds about right," said the first one who had spoken. "Killin' Wakefields seems to be in style round here, these days."

"In style thse days," the addlepated one chimed in.

"They call you Parrot, don't they?" Mallory asked the idjit, but didn't wait for a response. Facing the other, he went on, "And that makes you his brother Trenton, I believe."

"I guess we's famous," Trenton Wakefield sneered.

"Famous," Parrot repeated.

"You're confusing famous and notorious," said Mallory. "But I'll excuse that, since you likely never saw the inside of a schoolhouse."

"Didn't need no schoolin'," Trenton answered.

"Didn't need no—"

"Hush up, Parrot!" Trenton snapped.

"I'll jest hush up," Parrot agreed.

"What for you wanna bother us, Sheriff?" Trenton inquired. If he had ever looked thoughtful, Mallory guessed this must be it.

"Just wondering what brings you into town," he said.

"Free country, ain't it?"

"Funny you should say that, Trenton. I thought Wakefields loved the good old days of slavery."

"I wouldn't contradict you there, Sheriff. But we's *white* men, ain't we?"

"Might be, under that layer of grime you're wearing. Now, I'm gonna ask you simple, one last time. What brings you here?"

"You oughta know, Lawman," Trenton replied. "We come to make arrangements for our kinsmen what was murdered on the road."

"You mean the four who tried robbing the wrong stranger? I'd say they just ran out of luck, and high time, too."

"You *would* say that. But we still got a Christian right to bury 'em."

Mallory laughed aloud at that. "Did you say 'Christian'? That's a good one, coming outa your mouth."

"Hey! My mam taught me the fear of Jesus."

"Can you spell it?"

Trenton blinked and asked, "Spell what?"

"I don't care. Take your pick. Try 'the' or 'of'."

"You smart son of a—"

"Easy now, Trenton. You're rufflin' Parrot's feathers. Either one of you reach for a shootin' iron, I just might have to kill the both of you."

"You'd love that, wouldn't you?"

"It's not the worst idea I ever had," said Mallory. "Wouldn't exactly spoil my day."

"Well, if you's gonna *murder* us, get on with it. We seen the undertaker and we's just fixin' to leave when you delayed us. Shoot us if you wanna, all them witnesses with noses pressed against their windows. Others from my family might enjoy seein' a law dog hang."

"I checked the WANTED fliers at my office, and it doesn't look like either of you is on the run right now. Might take me fifteen, twenty minutes to convince Judge Kravitz that you both threatened an officer. Conviction means six months to one year on the county farm. You might pick up a useful trade between whippings."

"You don't scare us, Mallory," said Trenton.

"No? So, why's your Parrot sweating, then?"

"It's hot out here."

And Parrot could resist no longer. "Hot out here!" he seconded.

"It's cooler in the woods you came from," said the Sheriff. "If you're smart, you'll start riding right now and not come back."

"We'll have to fetch the bodies."

"Send somebody else. I doubt the pair of you could drive a wagon, anyhow."

Stiff-legged and resentful, Trenton climbed aboard a roan mare, while his brother mounted a flea-bitten gray. For just a second, Mallory thought Trenton might try riding over him and cocked both hammers on his scattergun, their *clack-clack* sounding loudly in the street.

When they were out of sight, Mallory eased the shotgun's hammers down and walked back to his office, careful to avoid the eyes of townspeople he passed along the way.

Main Street was quiet when Thorn got back from the freedmen's quarter, not a long ride, even though he felt as if he'd spanned two separate, conflicting worlds. It seemed to him that shoppers passing on the street and merchants tending to their wares found less to smile about than he had noted earlier, around Lake Village. And it didn't take him long to understand the reason why.

He found Sheriff Mallory awaiting him, when Gideon climbed down from Shadow's back and walked his horse into the livery. The hostler wasn't feeling jolly, either, but his face wasn't as sour as a few of those Thorn had observed along Main Street.

"It looks like someone rained on your parade, Sheriff," he said.

"A couple of 'em," Mallory replied. "Wakefields."

"Ah. Looking for me, I take it?"

"Not that they'd admit. Claimed they were in to see the undertaker about burying their kin. Makes sense, but I don't trust 'em any farther than a babe in arms can throw a full-grown hog."

"Well, it was bound to happen, I suppose."

"We'd better talk about it at my office when you're done here."

"Right. Should be about ten, fifteen minutes."

"I'll have coffee on," said Mallory.

Thorn made it to the sheriff's office in twelve minutes, by his pocket watch, and smelled fresh coffee percolating from the street outside. Before Mallory had a chance to speak, Gideon said, "You want me out of town, I won't raise any fuss. I just need time to pack my things and settle up at the Grandee."

"Hold on a second, there," said Mallory. "I haven't said a word about you goin' anywhere."

"Okay. What, then?"

Mallory poured two mugs of coffee, passing one to Thorn. "I warned 'em off, at least for now, but I can't promise you they won't be back with reinforcements. If they come—"

Thorn nodded, interrupting. "I don't need to be here. Fact is, I've already spoken to the people I was after. None of them admits to knowing anything about Dinah after she checked out of the Chicot House. It's like she just evaporated."

"I don't like the sound of that," said Mallory.

"Neither do I."

"Nothing from talking to Erasmus Jones?"

"He says she never got as far as seeing him, although it sounds like maybe he expected her."

"And you believe him?"

Thorn sipped coffee. Said, "I see no reason not to."

"Not unless he had something to do with it."

"I didn't get a guilty feeling from him, Sheriff."

"Now you sound like Jones, himself."

"We have a thing or two in common," Gideon acknowledged.

"And I'm guessing I don't wanna know what those might be."

"I'd say you're right."

"This whole thing... Christ, it's got me frazzled. I just don't know what to make of it."

"Nor I," Thorn said. "As to the Wakefield problem..."

"I'd prefer to keep the killin' out of town, if possible," said Mallory, "but that's their call, not mine. I'm not about to tell you that you can't defend yourself from harm. That's one thing this whole country's founded on, as I see it."

"But if they try something in town..."

"I'm with you," Mallory assured him. "Least ways, if I know about it soon enough to help, and no one picks me off before then."

"I appreciate that, Sheriff, but I won't be standing for election at the next term."

"Well, the people of Lake Village picked me out to keep 'em safe. I can't do that with Wakefields runnin' wild, while I send people outa town to get their heads blown off. What kinda sheriff would I be, at that?"

"I can't advise you on the politics," said Gideon, "and wouldn't if I could."

"Screw politics. Doin' the right thing has to count for something, doesn't it?"

"I hope so, but I'd hate to get you killed on my behalf or run out of your job."

"Let's wait and see what happens, eh? Don't like to borrow trouble when I've got enough already on my plate."

"That's why I thought—"

"Hey, don't go thinking on me, will ya? I already have your friend's weight on my shoulders, not paying enough attention when she was in town, much less pursuin' it when she dropped outa touch that way. When I imagine what her family's been going through..."

"I never heard her mention any living relatives," Thorn said. "I don't suppose that helps much."

"Precious little, truth be told. Damn shame Erasmus couldn't help at all."

"I wouldn't go that far," said Gideon. Though hesitant, he forged ahead. "You ever hear of zombies, Sheriff?"

"Hell, who hasn't? Least ways, living right next door to Loo'siana like we do. Talk's in the wind from colored folk. No way of missing it—which ain't the same as saying I *believe* it, now. Let's get that straight between us."

Thorn nodded but didn't answer right away. Frowning, Mallory said, "Hold on a sec, here. Are you tellin' me you think there's something to that Voodoo folderol?"

"I'm not sure, yet," Thorn said. "I've seen some strange things in my travels, but I wouldn't want to burden you with that."

"Sweet Jesus," said the sheriff. "No, I guess you'd better not."

Northeast of Lake Village

"That fat sumbitch," said Trenton Wakefield, slouching in his saddle. "I would purely *love* to let the air out of 'im."

"Air out of 'im," Parrot said right back.

"Thinks he can run us outa town that way and tell us that we better not *come back*? Who do he think he is?"

"Thinks he's the sheriff," Parrot answered, making sense for once.

"I *know* that, idjit! I mean... Fuck it! Never mind. We gotta tell the fambly, take a vote on what they wanna do."

"A vote."

"Damn right."

"What if they vote against ya?" Parrot asked.

"The hell's got into you?" asked Trenton.

"Into me?"

"Forget it. Trust me when I say the fambly ain't about to take this lyin' down. Four Wakefields lyin' in pine boxes, and the sheriff kicks *us* outa town, when all we wanna do is get the burial set up?"

"I thought we gone to kill that stranger, Trent."

"Well, *sure* we did. But Christ, the sheriff didn't know that, did he?"

"Um—"

"I'm tellin' ya he didn't know. He *couldn't*. Now he's made his self an enemy, same as that other piece a shit."

"We'll go back, then?" asked Parrot. "Maybe go tonight?"

"Don't set your heart on goin' with us, Baby Brother.

Maybe you ain't old enough to pull your weight on heavy duty."

"I's sixteen," Parrot protested.

"Comin' up next month, that is," Trenton corrected him. "Besides, it won't be up to me."

"Pap?"

"He'll have somethin' to say about it, bet your life. The stranger done bet his whole stake, and that's a losin' bet, for certain sure."

"I wanna he'p you do the sheriff, Trent."

"So? What you want and what'll happen might be diff'rent things."

"What if Pap says I can?"

Trent frowned and nodded. "No one votes against Pap," he granted. "Least ways, no one plannin' on longevity."

"Long what?" asked Parrot.

"That means livin' for a lotta years. Ain't never been a Wakefield specialty, as I recall."

"First time for ever'thing, ain't there?"

Trent laughed aloud at that, frightening crows out of the nearby trees. "You are a caution, Parrot. Hell, I gotta give ya that."

"A caution," Parrot echoed, sounding satisfied.

"You ever had a woman, Parrot? Or at least a girl?"

His younger brother blushed bright crimson underneath his coat of grime and muttered back, "Ya know damn well I ain't. Don't rub it in, will ya?"

"Nossir. But I was thinkin', if you get to ride with us when we go back to get the stranger and that sheriff, you might wanna try it once, before you hit the trail. You know...in case you don't come back,"

"Why wouldn't I..." Parrot caught on a second later, saying, "Damn. You mean in case they kill me?"

"Anything can happen on a raid, Brother. Ridin' into Lake Village like that, lookin' for blood, it might not be your night. Might not be *mine*."

"Don't say that, Trenton! Just you don't!"

"Forget it, Parrot. I'm just breakin' wind. It don't mean nothin'."

"Then you hadn't oughta say it!"

"I heard ya the first time. Christ all Friday, let it go, will ya?"

"Awright."

They rode along in silence for a while, then Parrot had to ask, "How many do ya reckon would be goin' on a deal like that?"

"At least four," Trenton answered. "Maybe five or six, if Pap reckons we need that many."

"Would *he* come with us?"

"Not likely. He'd have to be mighty riled to ride along, instead of sittin' back and givin' orders."

"Guess I'll jest keep my fingers crossed, then."

"And about that other thing I mentioned to ya..."

"What? You mean...the girl?"

"I don't mean Mam's ole blue tick hound."

"I don't know anybody that well," Parrot said. "Not well enough to ask 'em, anyways."

"Don't have to *ask*, do ya?"

"What else?"

"I hope you know what else. And if ya don't, you really is an idjit, Baby Brother."

"What? You mean just *tell* her?"

"Why let talkin' even enter into it?" asked Trenton.

"Shit, I don't know *sign* language, awright?"

"Damn fool. I mean remember you's a Wakefield, Parrot. Just *take* what you want."

"Last I heard, fellas get strung up for that."

"Does they?"

"Well..."

"What if the girl be black?" Trent asked.

Parrot seemed startled into silence for a moment, then he said, "I never thought a that."

"You never thought a lotta things. That's why ya got me lookin' out for ya."

"Still, I don't know..."

"We gotta pass right by the Quarter headin' home. You don't want any, Parrot, you can hold the horses while I get me some."

"Well, if you put it that way..."

"That's my boy. About to be a man."

LAKE VILLAGE

Gideon stopped into Bergeron's again for supper, got the same waitress, and found her just as friendly as before. He didn't recognize the other diners, and they weren't as smiley as the group last evening, but that was fine. By now, word of the Wakefield visit would've made the rounds, and smart people were second-guessing whether they should be so glad that Thorn was still in town.

To make a change from last night's fare, Thorn ordered filé gumbo, followed up with blackened alligator gar and *macque choux*, a side dish made of corn, bell pepper and onion, braised in a pot with stock and seasonings. Fried hush puppies took the place of bread, washed down with frosty beer that cooled Thorn's palate while he ate. He had a slab of cherry cobbler for dessert, and then a second beer instead if coffee, even though he didn't plan on sleeping much.

To let his meal settle, Thorn paid a final visit to the livery, wishing Shadow and Belle goodnight. If something happened and he didn't see them in the morning, Thorn supposed the animals would have to understand as best they could.

The Grandee's manager nodded at Thorn and said, "No messages today, Sir," before Gideon could ask. Thorn hadn't been expecting any—there was no reason Obi Magoro should've answered his last telegram—but for a moment he felt isolated, cut off from the wider world.

It was a feeling that he'd grown accustomed to during his travels, and it never seemed to get him down. Of course, this was the first time he'd gone looking for a person whom he knew, and he was getting nowhere fast.

Erasmus Jones had spooked him just a little, with his talk of zombies both alive and risen from the dead. Thorn couldn't scoff at that, after some of the other jobs he'd taken on, but now he had to think about what he could do for Dinah Pilcher if he found her in some kind of weird suspended animation—or if it was even worse than that.

"Goddamn it, Dinah," Thorn addressed his empty room. "Where are you?"

The room, of course, did not reply.

Thorn didn't know if there'd be Wakefields coming into town tonight, but he prepared his weapons, just in case, and started with the largest first. His 1872 Sharps rifle hurled bullets weighing twenty-nine grams down range at 1,750 feet per second, striking its target with 2,700 foot-pounds of explosive energy, enough to topple any living thing on Earth—and some, as Thorn had seen, that shouldn't be alive.

His smaller rifle, a lever-action Winchester Model 1873, held fifteen .44-40 cartridges in its tubular magazine, plus one in the chamber. That ammo also served his matched pair of Colt Single Action Army revolvers—the "Peacemakers"—giving Thorn an option of twenty-eight shots without reloading. Each slug weighed fourteen grams and left the weapon's muzzle traveling 1,200 feet per second.

And if things went badly, should he wind up fighting hand-to-hand, Gideon also had his two knives: a twelve-inch Bowie on his pistol belt, together with a smaller five-inch dagger, double-edged, kept in a boot sheath, within easy reach of his right hand. Nor was that all. If worse came to worst, he could fall back on Obi's training in hand-to-hand combat.

Whether he was packing guns or battling bare-handed, Thorn remained a lethal customer. The problem, he supposed now, would arise if his opponent was already dead.

Thorn hoped it wouldn't come to testing that hypothesis. Alas, he knew from long experience that he could take nothing for granted, whether it was ghosts, some ancient god intruding from a parallel dimension, prehistoric creatures "known" to be extinct—or simply homicidal madness generated by disordered human minds. In Thorn's time, he had faced them all, and he was still alive to tell the tale, assuming anybody might believe him.

Dinah Pilcher had, after she'd lived through two of Gideon's peculiar, deadly cases, and she'd meant to share his story with the world. He cared nothing about that wish of hers tonight, except if it had led her into peril of a nature still unknown.

The slaughter of his family when he was two years old had been beyond Thorn's power to prevent. But now, if

Dinah had been murdered or transformed to be a madman's mindless slave, Gideon wasn't sure he could ever forgive himself.

Meanwhile, if Wakefields came for him in search of vengeance, they might find they'd made the worst mistake of their pathetic lives.

SEVEN

YELLOW BAYOU, CHICOT COUNTY

"Awright, y'all settle down now," said Pap Wakefield, as he called the family gathering to order. When that didn't work, he raised his raspy voice, shouting, "I said shut the fuck up and that means all a ya!"

The nameless Wakefield settlement on Yellow Bayou was located six miles north-northeast of Lake Village, some eight miles west of the Mississippi River separating Arkansas from the Magnolia State next-door. It was the site of inconclusive skirmishing between rebels and bluecoats back in 1864, with neither gaining any ground, and its proximity to Mississippi made the land ideal fir running back and forth when trouble with the law grew too intense in one state or the other.

Finally, the group of twenty-five or so Wakefields, inside a barnlike structure sporting large holes in its roof, fell silent, all eyes fixed on Pap and Mam, seated together in a pair of rockers situated on a flatbed wagon. No one present could recall the last time they had seen the wagon move out of its present resting place.

"Y'all know why we's here," Mam said, her voice like ragged fingernails scraping across a chalkboard. "Some'un kilt four of our kin, a fancy bastard from up north some'ers, and then today, the goddamn sheriff run Trenton and Parrot outa town while they was lookin' to the funeral partic'lars."

Muttering began among the other Wakefields, long on cursing, short on any grammar that a schoolteacher might recognize.

"It be our duty," Pap chimed in again, "to pay them fuckers back for killin' and insultin' us like were was nothin' but some cowshit on they's boots."

More muttering, before Pap raised a calloused hand to still the racket. "Now," he said, "Trenton has got some infermentation to he'p us get the job done, so I need y'all to listen up. Trenton? Go on, now."

Trent stood up from the moldy hay bale he'd been sitting on and took off his slouch hat, baring a scalp that looked moth-eaten in the filtered light that came in from the holey roof. Clearing his throat and spitting for effect, he told his audience, "What Pap here says be true. That sheriff didn't show us no consideration for our loss and threatened to arrest us if we come back into town. O' course, he ain't locked up the sumbitch shot our kin, nossir. From what I heard, he even tried to give the bastard a reward in cash for killin' 'em."

"Weren't they wanted for somethin'?" Uncle Rufus asked from the backrow.

"That ain't the point, fer Christ's sake!" Pap replied on Trent's behalf. "We got our friggin' honor to uphold, don't we?" A chorus of assent greeted his words, urging him on.

"Somebody kills a Wakefield," Pap declared, "and *we* kill *them*. That ain't hard to remember, even if your brain's pickled on shine."

"Goddammit, I was just askin'," Rufus grumbled.

"Clam up!" Pap ordered. Then, to Trenton, "Go ahead on, boy."

"Yessir. We found out that the sumbitch did it calls hisself Gideon Thorn. He's stayin' at the Grandee there, in Lake Village."

"What room?" asked Mam.

"Nobody we run into knew that part," Trent answered back. "It's only got bout twenny rooms, though. Need be, we could burn the whole place down."

"I like your feelin' for revenge, boy," Pap said. "But we gotta do this smart like, nothin' that'd give ole pissant Miller up in Little Rock any excuse to send his damn militia pokin' into shit that don't concern 'im."

"So are we gonna get this prick or not?" one of their cousins, Cain Wakefield, inquired.

"We're gonna get 'im right enough," Pap said, "but we ain't all goin' in town to do it. Maybe five or six, but that's the limit."

Every man present stuck up a hand to volunteer, plus three of the women, all wearing faces more hard-bitten than their mates'. Pap scanned the group, delayed a moment, then began to speak again.

"First thing," he said, "I's sendin' Trent and Parrot, since they had to take the fat-ass sheriff's insult and bring back the word, instead of killin' him right there and maybe gettin' kilt theirselves."

"Parrot?" one of the older men challenged. "The hell's *he* gonna do if—"

"Shut it!" Pap ordered. "A boy's gotta become a man sometime."

"A man sometime," Parrot chirped from the audience.

"And I'll pick four more, one kinsman for each a them got murdered yestiddy. I'm choosin' Jackson...Brainerd...Willem...and...let's see...Garner."

Before the rejects had a chance to cut up rough about his choices, Pap talked over the beginnings of their grumbling. "Now, one question for ya, Trent."

"Whassat, Sir?" Trenton asked.

"I reckon you should tell us all what took the pair of you so all-fired long in gettin' back here with the news."

Trenton tried frowning as a pretense of confusion. "Sir?"

"Don't 'Sir' me now, boy. You heard me aright. Answer the goddamn question."

"Well, Sir—"

"You stall me again with 'Sir,' I'm gonna grab ya by the tongue and yank your innards outa ya."

"We made a little stop along the way, Pap. Goin' by the freedmen's quarter."

"Lollygaggin' with the niggers?" Mam chimed in. "The hell's wrong widya, boy?"

"Mam, I reckoned Parrot would be goin' in to put this right. Didn't seem right he'd have to shoulder that afore he was a man full-growed."

"You find a way to make 'im age quicker?" asked Pap.

"Kinda. We stopped to let 'im have a woman for the first time."

Laughter rippled through the audience at that, and Parrot blushed beet-red.

"A *woman* was it? And how old was she?" Pap asked.

"We didn't ask 'er," Trenton said.

"Now it's 'we,' is it? So you wasn't just doin' a favor for your brother."

"Well..."

"And here some a you reckoned Parrot was the dumb un," Pap replied.

"Now, Pap—"

"I'm gonna ask you one more time how old she were, and if ya give me any fuckin' lip..."

"I'd reckon twelve, thirteen."

"By which you mean ten, mebbe nine," Mam put in, scornfully.

"But just a nigger gal," Trenton replied, trying to justify himself.

"You leave her breathin'?" Pap demanded.

"Yeah, I guess."

"You *guess*?" Pap gowered at him for a long half-minute, then said, "Boy, since you was careless, you gone haveta clean that up afore it comes back on us. Understand me?"

"Yessir. I'll take care of it."

"You'll *both* take care of it, your little brother bein' man enough to make the mess."

"We'll do 'er, Pap."

"But first things first," Mam said. "We gotta wait for dark now, then take care of Mr. High-and-Mighty Thorn, what spilt the Wakefield blood. Do that and do it right, *then* finish cleanin' up your shit afore you come back home."

"Speakin' of first things first," Pap said, the night's activities planned out now, "who wants barbecue?"

LAKE VILLAGE

Thorn's watch told him it had gone half-past eleven, and the better part of Chicot County's seat was either sleeping soundly or preparing to. Its two saloons, the Busted Flush and Bayou Ben's were doing business on a par with last night's, from the sound of laughter and off-key piano music coming from behind their batwing doors. Main Street's half-dozen street lamps, lit up just around full dusk, cast as much shadow as they did light on the mostly-unused thoroughfare.

Gideon was awake and waiting by his window, the sash raised to admit any *clip-clop* of horses' hooves outside, bootheels clocking along the wooden sidewalks, or the murmuring of men who didn't want their conversations overhead.

And so far, nothing.

If the storm he'd been anticipating didn't break by midnight, Thorn decided he'd turn in and get some sleep. Across the way, he'd already seen Sheriff Mallory lock up his office, headed home on foot to wherever he lived, presumably on one of the backstreets. In passing, Mallory had glanced up at Thorn's lighted window, saw him sitting there, and raised one hand in a lazy salute.

Now Gideon was watching on his own, hoping he wouldn't need the weapons he'd prepared to welcome any Wakefields who stopped by.

At times like this, Thorn sometimes wished he smoked, if just to pass the time, but he had never gotten the tobacco habit and it seemed too late for him to start now—or just foolish, come to think of it. He took enough risks as it was, just traveling around and poking into things most folks would gladly leave alone. Why push his luck and wind up wheezing like a clapped-out locomotive well before his time?

Later, he'd curse himself for being less attentive than he should've been, missing some sign of trouble that he hadn't seen and hadn't heard. It made no sense to blame himself for that, but he could damned well blame himself for bringing trouble to Lake Village in his wake.

That was the kind of thing that haunts a man.

First thing, he heard a voice raised from the Grandee's lobby, one floor down. It was the night clerk, Howard Janeway, but Thorn couldn't tell exactly what he'd said. A gunshot smothered that, and then a rising wail of pain.

Gideon grabbed his Winchester, his gunbelt already strapped on, and stepped into the corridor outside his room. The wailing from downstairs had stopped by then, which could mean anything. Thorn knew he couldn't stop and think about the hotel's clerk right now, wouldn't allow himself to be distracted from the hard work of survival.

Footsteps started pounding up the stairs to reach his floor. Of course, the Wakefields would've known where he was staying, if they took the time to ask some citizen at one of the saloons. Thorn was a small-town hero of the moment in Lake Village, now about to change his stripes involuntarily and play the villain of the piece.

Whatever happened next, he thought, was absolutely down to him.

He'd moved halfway along the hall, closing his distance from the stairs, before the first intruder showed himself. He was a man of middle years, clutching a double-barreled shotgun to his chest and gaping when he saw they hadn't managed to surprise their target after all.

Gideon didn't hesitate, just shot him in the face and sent him tumbling back downstairs, some others shouting curses as they had to jump aside or take the ride down with him. That was Thorn's cue to advance with long, swift strides, working his rifle's lever-action as he went, the stock against his shoulder, peering down its barrel, looking for his next target.

There was a snarl-up on the stairs. The first man he had shot was stuck there, halfway down, after he'd run into another Wakefield's legs and got all tangled up in them. Beyond those two and lower down, a figure that he'd seen on Main Street earlier that day, one of their scouts, was angling a Colt Dragoon revolver at him, but his hand was shaking too much for him to aim properly.

Thorn drilled a blowhole through his concave chest and slammed him back into the lobby, just as shouting from Main Street began, the townsfolk rousted from their beds or from the barrooms by gunfire.

Gideon pumped the lever-action on his Winchester again as he descended, closing on a dead man and the live one whom he'd knocked ass-over-tea kettle. The live one saw Thorn coming, fired a wasted pistol shot into the wall, and shouted out to no one, "Jesus God!"

The gaping mouth gave Thorn a perfect target from a range of six feet, maybe less. Blood streaked the Grandee's wallpaper, and Gideon wondered how much the cleaning bill would run to.

By the time he reached the hotel's lobby, only one Wakefield remained, and he was racing toward the exit. Gideon lined up his rifle's sights and fired his fourth shot of the night, striking too low, but still it cracked the gunman's pelvis from behind and turned his legs to flopping rubber as he fell facedown.

How many more would they have sent? How many did he still have left to kill or maim?

Stopping before the registration desk, Thorn peered over its blood-streaked top and saw Janeway, still breathing from the look of him, but fading fast. He guessed there had to be a doctor living somewhere in the county seat, its only town of any size, but whether he'd arrive in time to help was anybody's guess.

Howard Janeway had lost a lot blood already, and his breathing was a gasping wheeze. Thorn guessed he wouldn't hang on for much longer, but eliminating any further Wakefield threat took top priority.

The hip-shot gunman on the lobby floor was groaning piteously as he tried to crawl outside, leaving a trail of murky fluid as a wounded giant snail might do. Gideon overtook him, kicked his fallen Henry rifle out of reach and plucked a six-gun from under his coat, tossing it aimlessly behind him as he left the Grandee, glancing carefully in each direction first.

Most of the customers from both saloons had spilled into the street, shouting, some of them pointing toward him on the sidewalk with his Winchester in hand.

"You're better off indoors," Thorn called to them, but left them to decide the matter for themselves. If alcoholic curiosity compelled them to approach, he couldn't let their presence on the battlefield distract him from his primary objective.

That was Wakefields, and Thorn saw a muzzle flash off to his left, the rifle's *crack* arriving a split-second later, as the bullet sizzled past him, taking out one of the Grandee's ornate windows. Ducking, Gideon thought, *Damn, they'll never let me back in here*, then went to hunt down his surviving enemy.

The alley was a pitch-dark deathtrap, but he guessed the man he hadn't shot yet would be fleeing for his life, knowing the others in his killing party must have come to grief. He hadn't seen the second Main Street watcher from that afternoon, and couldn't say how many shooters had been sent in total for the kill. Whatever, there was still at least one Wakefield skulking around Lake Village, and maybe more.

Gideon crossed Main Street at an oblique angle, reaching the alley half a minute later, lingering that long again before he plunged into the darkness, moving in a crouch. There were no street lamps at the other end, but moonlight worked nearly as well, revealing no bushwhackers waiting in the shadows there.

Thorn did, however, pick up sounds of horses circling, getting set to run.

Abandoning caution, he ran along the alley's length and cleared it just in time to see two horsemen riding off, both hunched over their saddles, lashing with their reins to call up greater speed. He froze in place and picked the larger of the two retreating riders, lining up his Winchester and squeezing off with cold deliberation that felt desperately slow.

His man pitched from the saddle, landing in a crumpled heap, and Gideon allowed the last survivor to escape. It was a dicey shot for nighttime, and he thought it wouldn't hurt to have the other Wakefields ponder on their folly in attempting to assassinate him.

That is, if they had the wits to learn from their mistake.

Winchester tucked beneath his arm, he started back toward Main Street and the angry questions that he knew awaited him.

NORTH OF LAKE VILLAGE

Parrot Wakefield couldn't stop bawling over his brother's death, no matter how he tried. It pained his innards, as he thought it might've hurt if he'd been shot, himself.

And there was abject fear, as well. Parrot wasn't exactly sure how Pap and Mam would turn the slaughter of their kin around and make it all his fault, but he was damned sure that they wouldn't take responsibility for what had happened on themselves, even though Pap had chosen who to send and now five of the six were dead as doornails. Would they want to kill *him* for it, maybe banish him from Yellow Bayou, which amounted to the same thing? Could he maybe get by with a whipping that would leave him flayed and only wishing he could die from it?

One thing Parrot was certain of: he had to get back home and tell the family, no dawdling around with some distraction like he had that afternoon.

Thinking about the colored gal they'd messed with set Parrot to weeping once again. He wasn't sure why that should be, hadn't been raised to think of her people as human, but the way she'd carried on when it was happening, it almost made him think she had a soul inside her, just like anybody else.

With that in mind, Parrot considered lighting out, not even going home at all, but that was stupid—something that his kinfolk might expect an idiot to do. All right, Parrot knew he was slow and didn't talk so well, couldn't string words together properly or even think of them himself, most times, but he was smart enough to know he couldn't make it on his own, not in the outside world. He needed someone showing him the way, telling him what to do, or at the very least, helping him work it out himself.

He had another three, four miles to go on his flea-bitten gray, but wasn't sure about the distance after nightfall. That was typical, talking to Trenton and the others while the rode from Yellow Bayou into Lake Village, not studying the landmarks so he'd recognize them later, in the dark.

And now, he'd never see Trenton again, at least not living, wouldn't hear him calling Parrot "Baby Brother," treating him as if he had the right to live and wasn't just some creature from the swamp that always made mistakes and couldn't figure why.

What would he do without his brother? How would he survive?

Up ahead, Parrot saw movement in the shadows on the left side of the trail. He slowed his mount and pulled the pistol from his belt, a Colt Navy Revolver borrowed from the Wakefield arsenal just for tonight, since Pap and Mam didn't think Parrot could be trusted with a full-time shooter of his own.

His hand was quaking as he cocked it and called out, "I seen you there. Come out 'n lemme see those hands!"

Someone came out, all right, and not just one of them, but three. They were all nigras, but he'd never seen their people move so slow and awkward-like, even when they were dragging ass and shirking in the cottonfields. One of them had a straw hat on, the other two bare-headed. If he'd wanted to described their clothing, Parrot would've said they'd dressed in rags, and none of them were wearing shoes.

The trio shuffled toward him, fanning out a bit to block the narrow road. Parrot, outnumbered, wondered whether he could drop all three of them before they rushed him, but the thought of rushing anywhere seemed to escape them, whatever they had in mind for him.

"Awright, y'all. I mean to pass, and if you's smart, you'll stand aside. Don't make me let the moonlight through ya, now!"

The warning seemed to fall on deaf ears. Parrot tried to figure out which one he should shoot first, but then they *did* decide to rush him, one on each side of his gray, the middle one loping directly toward his horse with arms outstretched, trying to hug it tight around the shoulders, underneath its throat.

"Goddamn you stupid nig—"

Before he had a chance to finish it, the one in front had stopped his gray somehow, while those to Parrot's right and left were clutching at his legs, pulling with an uncanny strength for men who looked as famished, downright feeble, as they did. Their fingers gripped the fabric of his trousers, pulling him in opposite directions without any vestige of cooperation to remove him from his saddle.

"Shit!" Parrot jabbed at the upturned face below him, on his right, and pressed the Colt's muzzle against the dark forehead. He fired without thinking, the recoil jolting up along his arm, and Parrot saw his adversary's skull cap come apart.

The dead man still kept hold of him, kept pulling, even though he should've vaulted over backwards—and now what in hell was Parrot seeing? Was it just a trick of moonlight and his panic, or was that a mass of worms seething where he expected shattered brains to be?

A sudden *ripping* in his groin made Parrot screem and drop his pistol, groping for his saddle horn to keep himself aboard the gray and upright, but it didn't help. A rush of hot blood filled his trousers as the nightwalkers each backed away with one of Parrot's legs in opposite directions, while be blead out, "Trenton!"

LAKE VILLAGE

"My Lord," said Sheriff Mallory, not praying, simply at a loss for words as he surveyed the Grandee's blood-spattered interior. "I never saw the likes of this, at least not since the war."

Thorn made no comment, thinking it would be a bad time to remind the lawman that they'd spoken of an outcome just like this when it was still daylight, and Mallory refused to send him on his way. Outside, townspeople drifted past the front of the hotel in twos and threes, most of them looking stunned.

"You say there's still another one off yonder, over that way?" Mallory's left arm waved vaguely to the west, beyond Main Street,

"Two," Thorn corrected him. "I shot one off his horse as they were riding out. He should be lying where he fell unless coyotes have been after him."

"Could be red wolves around here," Mallory said. "O' course, they're not red, but... Forget it. Are you tellin' me one got away?"

"I am. He was beyond effective range, and anyway, I'd tired of killing them by then."

"I see how that could happen."

"How's Janeway?" Gideon asked.

"You saw Doc Alward and the others take him outa here. It looks bad, all that blood he lost, but he might make it, I suppose. The rest of these...

The Wakefield who had tried to drag himself outside was dead when Thorn came back from chasing his accomplices, a pool of dark blood spreading under him.

"Reckon they'll haveta take these floorboards up, along with all the rest of it," Mallory mused.

Thorn nodded, saying, "I can foot the cost of that, Sheriff. I'm not without resources."

"Never mind that now. Just walk me through what happened, so our undertaker can get busy hauling out these stiffs."

Thorn had already sketched the action for him in a few short sentences, but he went into greater detail now: the night clerk shouting from behind his desk and getting shot; Thorn waiting for the first man up the stairs and dropping him, then coming down and picking off the others on the staircase, in the lobby, finally his journey down the alley and what followed it.

"So, five of 'em," said Mallory, "plus one that got away."

"That's all I saw," Gideon said. "If they had other spotters, backup standing by, they slipped away without me noticing."

"Wakefields." Mallory spoke the name as if it were a malediction. "Not a one of 'em went off to fight during the war. Cowards, the scurvy lot of 'em. They played tag with patrols along the border, hunting slackers and deserters, from the start of it in '61 right on to Appomattox. Both before and since then, they've been livin' off the land and whatever they get from robbin' travelers or breakin' into homes when no one's there. I wish their men had all been caught and shipped off to the army then, or shot for shirking duty. Woulda saved us all a world of trouble."

"All of these were Wakefields, then?" Thorn asked, when Mallory ran out of steam.

"Oh, yeah. That's Garner that you got first, and his cousin Brainerd, tangled up with Garner on the stairs. Next one in line is Trenton, from this afternoon. This one"—

Mallory nodded toward the body lying near the doorway —"used to be Jackson. I'll have to check the one fell off his horse after you shot him, but he'll be a Wakefield too, no doubt."

"They don't run with a larger gang?" asked Thorn.

Mallory shook his head. "There's never been a sign of it. Two reasons I can think of. First, they think their blood is somethin' special, though you'd never know it, watchin' it dry on the walls and floor, would you? They don't trust anybody else, and by the same token, nobody else trusts *them*. The only thing that you can count on Wakefields for is helping one another, screwing everybody else."

That seemed to spark a memory that made the sheriff scowl. He said, "Which now reminds me. Not long after Trenton and his little brother left this afternoon, a woman from the freedmen's quarter came to see me. Said a couple low-life white trash got hold of her little girl and...well, use your imagination. No one saw 'em but the kid, and white men all look pretty much alike to her. I wondered if it might be Trent and Parrot—"

"Parrot?" Gideon thought he'd misunderstood the lawman.

"All I ever heard him called," said Mallory. "He's likely got a legal name, but who knows?" As an index finger tapped his skull, the sheriff said, "He's soft up here. Don't talk much, but repeats what others say like one of those trained birds."

"He would've been the one with Trenton earlier, on Main Street."

"That was him, all right. I don't know whether Pap and Mam would send him on a raid like this, dumb as he is, but if they *did*, he might turn out to be the fifth one you picked off."

"If you need me to see the judge or something..."

"Nah, forget about it. This was clear-cut self-defense, helping protect Lake Village from marauders."

"Even so. I can pack up my things and find someplace to camp outside of town until I'm finished here."

Mallory blinked at him, as if surprised, then said, "To hell with that. I live alone. It's not much of a place, but you can stay with me until you find out more about your friend."

"You're sure about that?"

"Hey, why not? What can these folks do to me now, but vote me out? Way things are headed, that might come as a relief."

EIGHT

LAKE VILLAGE: MARCH 15, 1877

At Sheriff Mallory's suggestion, they hit Bergeron's for breakfast, ordering an andouille sausage scramble with pan-fried potatoes on the side and toast that turned out to be sourdough. Thorn imagined that the other customers, whose looks were more in line with the suspicion he expected from small towns along his winding road, might well have been more openly hostile if Thorn had come in on his own, without the county sheriff at his side.

And now he had to wonder whether Mallory's next reelection bid would suffer—maybe fail—because of his public association with the man in black who'd rated smiles and handshakes yesterday.

Thorn hoped not, but one thing he'd never mastered was reversing time's grim course.

Before they'd gone to sleep last night, Thorn on the sheriff's sagging couch, he knew the last man he had shot last night was Willem Wakefield, one of the swamp-dwelling clan who had a WANTED poster out on him for robbery and manslaughter. As he was turning in, Mallory told him, "That's another purse you could collect. Not much, but still, three hundred bucks."

"Just lump it with the rest," Thorn said, "or put it toward repairs at the Grandee. I'll sign whatever papers are required."

"Your choice. I'll run it by Judge Kravitz when I get back into town, tomorrow."

"Back from where?" Thorn asked, as Mallory was blowing out his lamps.

"To Yellow Bayou. That's the spot Wakefields call home, of late. I have proof positive against them for the raid. Whether we find them, well, that's something else. One thing they know is how to run and hide."

Now, over breakfast, Thorn asked his companion, "When you mentioned going out today, you spoke of 'we.' Who's that include?"

"Not sure yet," Mallory replied. "You're welcome if you wanna ride along. Nobody else in Chicot County's put more Wakefields in the ground than you, far as I know."

"I'm thinking that's a reason why I *shouldn't* come. If you catch up with them, they're likely to be riled enough without the sight of me."

"I see your point. That means I'll have to ask around, see who can spare the time to join a posse other than the usual hung-over barflies."

"Well..."

"No, no. You're right," said Mallory. "If I take you along and it all goes to hell, I won't just lose the next election. I could wind up on the county road gang."

"Anyway," Thorn said, "I need to get away from Wakefields for a while and back to tracking Dinah."

"Any thoughts on how?" the sheriff asked.

"First thing, I'd like to take a ride around some of your local farms, plantations, whatever you call them in the South."

"To see what?"

"No idea," Thorn said. "I'll hope to recognize it if I spot it, though. Also, I thought I'd take a look at where your poacher died. Lake Boggy Bayou, was it?"

"That it was," said Mallory. "You'll likely need a guide, though, and you'll definitely need a skiff. Know how to handle one?"

"The basics," Gideon replied. "If I need help, I'd have to know he's trustworthy."

"So, not a Wakefield-lover, then."

"Not even close."

"Nobody much in town likes them, but just to be safe, I can name a couple boys I'd trust, before I go."

"Appreciate it, Sheriff."

That brought a shrug from Mallory. "I reckon we're still in this thing together, more or less. Your friend went missing on my watch, or near enough to make me feel regretful. Nothing else that I can do to help you if she left the county. If she didn't..."

Thorn spoke the words he dreaded. "Then she's likely dead by now."

"Mixed up with Voodoo or the Wakefields, either way, it's not a ticket to longevity."

"I had a fair idea about the odds before I got here," Gideon replied.

"Don't make it any easier though, does it."

"Not a bit."

"At least you know it wasn't *your* fault, right?"

Thorn nodded, but he still wasn't convinced. Their first adventure had been unavoidable, given the circumstances, and Dinah had asked herself along on the second. Then, like a fool, he had agreed to tell her his full story, let her set it down in writing, even publish it—and all for what? His ego didn't need the stroking, but he couldn't stop thinking that he'd put Dinah on the danger path full-time, which absolutely brought her here, 1,700 hundred miles from home, where she had very likely lost her life.

"We'll, I'm done here," said Mallory, as he pushed back his nearly spotless plate.

"Me, too. I'll take those guides' names, if you don't mind."

"Sure thing. They're Russell Long and Deke McMurtry —short for 'Deacon,' but he's not a gospel shouter. Ask around the livery to see where they'll be found."

"Thanks." Gideon left ample money on the table, and at least the waitress flashed a smile at him before he followed Mallory outside, into the sun.

NORTHEAST OF LAKE VILLAGE

Mallory found five men willing to ride along with him in search of Wakefields: Zephania Osborn, part-time hunting guide and trapper; Chauncey Ross, a handyman who mostly worked around the courthouse; Noel Torbee, from the Stanwyck feed store; Rudy Ragsdale, a part-timer at the Busted Flush; and Troy Blodgett, a blacksmith's helper. All of them were well armed for the hunt, and several of them harbored grudges against Pap Wakefield's menagerie.

Their goal was Yellow Bayou, as he'd told Thorn over breakfast, but they had some trouble getting there. First, Mallory had to collect the members of his posse, talk some of them into going for the county's pittance of a half-dollar per day, then wait for all of them to fetch their guns and horses, say good-bye to wives—except in Osborn's case, a lifelong single man—and then get started on the road. By then, it had been pushing ten o'clock, and Mallory supposed that any Wakefield who was sober and could mount a horse would be long gone.

Still, the only thing that he could offer anybody was his best effort.

Approximately three miles out of town and making decent time at last, they came on Parrot Wakefield—or, amending that, what there was left of him.

"Jesus, what happened to 'im?" Ross asked no one in particular.

"He's been split like a wishbone," Torbee answered for the rest of them, and no one could dispute it.

From the look of Parrot—and it was him, Mallory confirmed; there was enough left of his stupid-looking face to prove it—someone or some*thing* had grabbed him by the feet and pulled in opposite directions till he'd come apart below his narrow waist. At that point, his left leg had come away from the remainder of him and was lying over on the west side of the road, in bloodstained weeds. What happened after that, the sheriff couldn't say with any certainty, but those were clearly bite marks on both legs, where trouser fabric had been torn away, more of them on his arms and up around his neck.

Mallory's next question: what on God's Earth made bites like those on a man?

"I'm gonna puke!" Ragsdale announced, and hopped down from his saddle just in time to prove it, should the others doubt his word. Mallory turned away, not anxious to find out what Rudy'd had for breakfast.

From his long woodland experience, Osborn opined, "No bear that ever lived around these parts did that, I guarantee."

"What then?" asked Mallory.

Zeph shrugged. "A couple panthers coulda tussled with 'im, but they nearly always hunt alone, and them ain't panther bites, nor any other animal's I've seen afore."

Narrows it down, thought Mallory. *My ass, it does.*

"He didn't walk out here from town," the sheriff said, one thing he *could* be sure of. "He was seen riding away."

"So, where's his horse?" asked Blodgett.

"Tracks go off the way he was already headed," Osborn told them, pointing to the road, where Mallory, frankly, couldn't distinguish between one faint line of hoof prints and the rest, made over time. Still, it could fit.

"Back home, toward Yellow Bayou," he observed. "Awright, now. Someone has to double back and notify Joe Ettinger"—him being Chicot County's coroner—along with Roscoe Cagle. Have him come out here and haul this back to town. There'll have to be an inquest."

All five hands were in the air before he finished speaking. Mallory decided Ross would be the least useful if they ran into any further trouble and said, "That's you, Chauncey. No stopping off at either one of the saloons before you talk to 'em."

"No, Sir!" Ross said and wheeled his horse around toward town without a fare-thee-well.

"The rest of us are goin' on as planned," Mallory told his other posse members. "Keep your weapons handy, just in case, but don't go shooting one another, now."

WEST OF LAKE VILLAGE

Thorn rode out with no set goal in mind, nothing he could've called an actual itinerary. He'd left off for later hunting up a bayou guide, in case he came up empty on his ride along the roads around Lake Village, flanked by cotton fields on either side.

He'd studied botany at Harvard and was more or less aware of dates for planting and for harvesting the major crops in any given part of the United States. He knew, for instance, that in Arkansas the corn was mostly harvested in April and October, with the same dates typically applied to cotton. It should be six weeks he calculated, give or take, before the spring harvest concluded, but the fields weren't idle now. Long rows of men and women—white and black, all poorly dressed, with lean and hungry looks—were busy in amongst the rows, weeding, hoeing and making preparations for the main event.

Bosses on horseback moved among the workers, no whips dangling from their saddle horns as they would have back in antebellum times, but still barking commands if anyone seemed to be lagging, shirking what they had been paid their daily pittance to achieve. Some of the workers paused to watch Thorn riding past, before a field boss caught them at it and called out a reprimand. Watching them sweat, Gideon thanked his lucky stars—not for the first time—that he had been born to old money without knowing it, till his parents had been snatched away from him.

One of the larger spreads he passed was different. There was a wagon in the field, a water barrel standing in its flat bed, but he saw no supervisors lording over workers with their Stetsons on and rifles in their saddle boots. In this field, as he cantered past on Shadow, nearly all the field hands paused and straightened up from their backbreaking labor, turning to observe him on the road.

One thing Gideon noticed, even from a distance, was that black or white, male or female, none of them seemed to study him with anything approaching curiosity. Rather, they watched him as caged beasts might eyeball strollers at a zoo, secure in the knowledge that he wouldn't try to harm them—and that they could not reach him.

Thorn made a mental note to ask the sheriff whose plantation this was, and to back that up, if he felt so inclined, with yet another trip to see Erasmus Jones. Gideon couldn't put his finger on whatever tweaked his senses, feeling those eyes follow him, but there was something...

It must have been a mere passing conceit, he thought, that made wish they'd turn back to their work and cease staring at him.

That thought had barely taken shape in Thorn's mind when a bell chimed somewhere on the property, beyond his line of sight, likely up at the owner's house, and everyone laid down their hoes at once, moving in calm, orderly fashion to the wagon where a porky man in blue denim began to dole out metal cups of water from his keg.

The momentary spell broken, Gideon urged Shadow to greater speed and put the place behind him, moving on toward the next spread in line. A few more places, not many, and he would head back into town, seeking one of the guides that Sheriff Mallory had recommended over breakfast.

It was getting on toward time, he thought, to have a look at the bayou where Asa Daughtrey had been killed and bitten to the bone. That was one trip he didn't want to make after sundown, until he had a better take on what in hell was happening.

And while he looked for the solution to a mystery, he'd also keep a sharp eye out for Wakefields on the prod.

YELLOW BAYOU

"Looks like they done skedaddled," Zephania Osborn said.

"Good thing for them," said Troy Blodgett, voicing commendable courage now that it seemed there'd be no shooting after all.

As he surveyed the seedy bayou village, Sheriff Mallory saw no reason to question what they'd said, but still reminded them, "We have to check all through the buildings, anyhow."

"Watch out for lice," cracked Noel Torbee.

"Or booby traps," the sheriff said, bringing them back to Earth. "And snipers, too."

That got them looking warily around at walls of pine, oak, and bald cypress, most of the trees bearded with Spanish moss. The lower plants, still capable of hiding enemies, included coneflowers, spiderwort, climbing magnolia, and banks of ferns.

All looking nervous now, the four remaining members of his posse dismounted and secured their horses, followed by the sheriff as they fanned out toward the hovels that comprised the Wakefields' nameless settlement. They went from door to door, guns cocked and ready, ultimately coming up with what Zeph Osborn had suggested earlier: nothing and nobody.

"Cleared out and cleaned out," Rudy Ragsdale said,

emerging from a structure larger than the rundown shacks, more on the order of a long-abandoned barn. "Just rats and such in there."

"Whadda we do now, Sheriff?" Torbee asked.

"Nothing to do," said Mallory, "unless we go ahead and chase 'em to the Mississippi line."

"You wanna do that," Osborn answered, "I can likely track 'em. They'd a pulled out in a hurry, and I've never known a Wakefield smart enough to hide 'is trail."

"I worry more about an ambush," Mallory replied. "They take us by surprise in there—" he gestured broadly toward the marshy bayou country—"and we're done for. I ain't payin' you enough to get shot up from here to Sunday week."

"Damn straight," one of them muttered, likely Ragsdale.

"What we *could* do," Troy suggested, "is set light to all a this. At least make sure if they come creepin' back, they won't have any shelter waitin' for 'em."

"Look around, boys," Mallory replied. "I know this is a bayou, but a fire like that could catch ahold and spread for miles. The wind's right, it could even double back toward town."

"What, then?" Torbee inquired.

"How bout the next best thing?" asked Mallory. "Most of these shacks are barely standing as it is. We could use ropes and horse power to pull 'em down."

"That way, they still come back to nothin', should they come at all," Zeph Osborn said. "I like it."

Certain of the others didn't, but they set about the grunt work anyway and got it done within an hour and a half. In retrospect, Mallory thought, the makeshift Wakefield settlement hadn't deserved a name.

When they were done and mounted, ready to withdraw, Blodgett gave voice to what Malllory guessed that most of his companions must be thinking. "Now, suppose they *do* come back," he said, "and see all this. What are they gonna think?"

"That they should slink away and foul some other county," Osborn answered him.

"But think about it." Troy pressed on. "Won't they just see all this and get a mad on? Maybe come around and try to do the same thing to Lake Village?"

"Pull it down, you mean?" asked Mallory. "I doubt there's enough Wakefields living to tear down my office, much less the whole county seat."

"But if they *try,*" Blodgett kept on. "They're nuts enough to sneak around, set fires, and *they* won't give a rat's ass where that spreads to."

"So, you wanna stay behind and put 'em all back up again?" asked Ragsdale, nodding toward the flattened structures.

"Nope. I'm just sayin' that if they *do* come back—"

"They'll wish they hadn't," Sheriff Mallory spoke up, cutting him off. "We're goin' back now. Keep your fingers crossed that Roscoe has what's left of Parrot boxed and headed back to town when we get there."

NINE

WASHINGTON COUNTY, MISSISSIPPI

Safe across the state line, Pap and Mam Wakefield convened their family on wooded land that had provided shelter for them since the outbreak of the War Between the States. They'd been draft-dodgers then, and brigands always, well schooled in the rules of legal jurisdiction, if in nothing else but theft and homicide.

Their flight from Yellow Bayou was a family embarrassment, but nothing that they hadn't been through time and time again. Outlaws lived best when they were on the move. They died or went to prison when they tried to stop somewhere and put down roots.

Pap called the conference together by whacking his cane against a tree trunk, keeping at it till the others settled down and shut their mouths. Sometimes they irritated him as much as Wakefields raised the ire of so-called "decent folks," but they were still his kin. Their blood flowed through his veins; their need for vengeance lit a fire inside his paunch.

"We've lost ten men now, in the past two days," he told them, just in case some of the dumber ones had lost count on the road. "Since Parrot didn't make it home, we reckon he's among them murdered by this Yankee that come down here to raise hell right in our own backyard."

Growling sounded at that, and Pap gave them a minute to relieve themselves of anger before speaking up again. "Now fat-ass Sheriff Mallory might tell himself he's run us off, but I say he's dead wrong!"

That got a couple of "Amens," though Pap doubted that any of his kin had ever set foot in a church. One even clapped his hands, as if he thought Pap was some kind of play actor on stage.

"I never read the Bible," he continued. "Never learnt to read at all, in fact, but I recall the bit about takin' an eye for an eye and a tooth for a tooth."

More murmurs of assent, before he shouted at them, "Well, I say, fuck that! Some bastard pulls one o' your kinsmen's teeth, you rip 'is goddamn jaw off! If he plucks an eye, you leave him lyin' headless in the dirt!"

Hoots of agreement now, as Pap pressed on.

"In our world, there's no forgivin' nothin' and there's no forgettin'. We live by the *feud,* brothers and sisters, cousins, sons and daughters. When ya lay a hand on one Wakefield, the rest rise up to strike ya down. That's how it's always been, and how it always will be. Am I right?"

"You're *goddamned* right," his second cousin Ezra shouted, and the whole collection of them cheered, some waving knives and pistols overhead.

"Now, I got common sense enough to know we can't just turn around and go back into Lake Village *today,* but as God is my witness, we *are* goin'. And our enemies will rue the day they sheltered any stranger run afoul of us, much less a stinkin' Yank!"

Foot stomping from his kinfolk as he finished, and a rousing rebel yell from uncle Titus, all the way in back.

"So, here's how it's gonna be," Pap said, brooking no argument. "We lay up here tonight, and then we make our way back cautious-like. Nobody's gonna see us comin' till we's right on top o' them, cuttin' their throats and bashin' out their brains. I don't care if they's man, woman, or child. When we get through with 'em, there won't be no damn county seat or any trash to sit on it."

Cheering and clapping echoed through the dappled forest glade at that.

"Awright, you menfolk see about your weapons. Make sure all your guns is loaded, whet your knives, hatchets, and razors, while our womenfolk get supper on. We eat, then post guards through the night and sleep in shifts. First light, we head back to our rightful home. If we can't live there, nor can they. We'll let 'em feed the buzzards first!"

That said, Pap hobbled toward a tree stump he had picked out for himself and sat to watch the others do his bidding. Fair was only fair.

LAKE BOGGY BAYOU

"So, this is where you picked up Asa Daughtrey?" Gideon had learned that much from Deke McMurtry while they haggled over how much he would pay to see the killing site.

"Me 'n my friend Jake Caruthers," Deke replied. "We hunt 'n fish together sometimes, after this 'n that."

"He was just floating out here, then?"

As Thorn was speaking, he observed an alligator, ten feet long at least, slide off the bayou's mossy eastern bank, vanish beneath the gray-green water, then resurface forty-odd feet distant as a disembodied pair of knobby eyes, the rest of it invisible.

"We seen his skiff, first," said McMurtry, "and we recognized it right off. Called to 'im a couple times as we was paddlin' over to it, then he just bobbed up in front of us, all gassy, bloated white."

"That must have been...surprising," Gideon replied.

"Ah, nothin' that we hadn't seen afore. People come out this way to hunt, whatever, and they don't always come back. Tore up like Asa was, we knew he never had a chance."

"You don't think that an alligator could've done it?"

"*Coulda,* maybe, but it *didn't.*"

"You sound positive about that," Thorn observed.

"The thing about gators, they'll kill ya if ya give 'em half a chance, and eat ya in their own way, but their jaws is made for crushin', rippin', not for chewin' like we do. They don't got any of them teeth like we got—whatcha-call-'em, big ones at the back?"

"Molars?"

"That's it. So, gators might could tear a leg off, but they can't just *eat* it then, without they gulp it whole and maybe choke on it. Instead, they'll drag their big kills—man, deer, panther—underwater, hold it down until they's sure it's dead, then stash it underneath a log, or maybe down below the bank somewhere. They let the water *tenderize* it, then come back and feed before the turtles or whatever get the best or it."

"And that wasn't how Mr. Daughtrey died?"

"Not even close. The sheriff reckons somethin' *choked*

him, like a man would do, but he had bite marks on him, too. Not gator bites, with them sharp teeth, but kinda round in shape like someone bit into an apple or a wedge of cheese."

"When you say *someone*..."

"Yeah, I know. You think I lost my mind, eh?"

Thinking back to other corpses he had seen, Thorn answered quickly, "Not at all."

"You don't?"

Instead of answering a second time, Thorn changed the subject. "I was told that Mr. Daughtrey fought his killer."

"Fought like holy hell," McMurtry said.

"Fired off his rifle, and a pistol, too?"

"Not only *fired*. I guarantee he *shot* whatever took him down. Used that old Springfield .58 he brought home from the war, plus all six loads from his revolver."

"But he could have missed..."

"No, Sir. We found his rifle in the skiff, and it still had a piece of burnt skin stuck around its muzzle, where he pressed it right against whatever came for him. His pistol was right there beside it in the skiff, all six rounds fired. Couldn't a been more than a yard from whatever come after him. I've been on hunts with Asa, and he never missed nothin' that close to him with either shootin' iron."

"But if the bullets didn't stop it..."

"Way it looked to me, another somethin' or some*body* came up on his blind side, from behind, and took 'im down while he was squeezin' off his last shot from the six-gun. He was unarmed then, except a skinnin' knife he used to carry on his belt, but if ya can't protect yourself with seven shots point-blank, what good's a little blade?"

"You've got a point," said Gideon.

"Damn right I do." Deke hesitated, then went on. "Ya

know, this is the first time I been out here since we found him. Jake won't come out neither. Do our huntin' on dry land these days, although the prizes ain't as lush. They ever catch whatever did for Asa, mebbe I'll come back sometime. I wouldn't swear to that, though. Have to wait and see."

"Sounds wise," Thorn said.

"You seen enough, then?"

"Plenty," Gideon replied. "And thank you."

"Never mind that. You already paid me. Truth is, I'll be glad to get back into town and spend my earnin's at the Busted Flush."

"Have one on me," said Gideon.

"I'll have as many as I reckon I can hold, long as nobody has to cart me home like I's a sack 'o grain."

LAKE VILLAGE

By the time the got back into town and Gideon gave Deke an extra tip for beer or supper, he discovered that the sheriff's posse had returned from Yellow Bayou. Stopping by the lawman's office, he found Mallory behind his desk, hands on the blotter before him, fingers interlaced.

"It this a bad time?" Thorn inquired.

"I can't foresee a better one," said Mallory. "In fact, we may have seen our last good time round here until who knows when."

"No Wakefields out at Yellow Bayou, then?"

"One on the way out to it. Parrot," said the sheriff, reaching up to tap his temple with an index finger. "Simpleton, he was. Now something's caught him on the road and torn him limb-from-limb."

"Like Asa Daughtrey?"

"Worse." Mallory shook his head. "I can't to blaming gators or some other scavenger this time. Something took hold of his two feet and *ripped* him. There's no other way to say it. Roscoe Cagle and Doc Alward are together with 'im now, down to the mortuary, tryin' to decide what creature on God's Earth could do a man that way."

"And he was armed, like Daughtrey?"

"Found a pistol lyin' on the road beside where he went down, before his horse took off and made a run for it. I guess it got away, unless something went after it and kilt in the woods, back from the road. Might not have seen it, then."

"The cause of death?" asked Thorn.

"I'll leave that to the experts, but from what I saw, it coulda been a grab bag. Blood loss definitely was a factor, and there woulda been gross damage to his innards, down below the waist. I'm hopin' he was dead before whatever did it started gnawin' on 'im."

"Like the poacher?"

"Minus time spent in the water with the fish or whatever helpin' themselves to bits and pieces. Parrot was a dimwit, probably a criminal, bein' a Wakefield born and raised, but Christ, to die like that...I wouldn't that kinda death on anybody but the ones that killed him."

"You say 'ones'..."

"No question. Any less than two things couldn't grab 'im like was done, and even then, they'd have to be as strong as Hercules to rip someone in two like that, even a callow boy."

"So human, would you say?"

"You wanna call it that. The truth is...I don't know."

"But still, with hands and fingers, though."

"Looks like it, from the bruising. Still..."

"So not a bear, or anything like that."

Mallory shook his head. "Not any animal I know of in these parts," he said. "A bear, whatever, would take hold using its jaws. I guess..."

"What?"

"Nah, it's stupid."

"Tell me anyway."

"I was about to say one of them giant apes might do it, but we'd have to live in Africa or wherever they are.

"Gorillas?"

"Right, but it would still take two of 'em, one holdin' onto each of Parrot's feet. I might buy one of 'em escaping from a carnival or some such. Two of 'em, no way."

"We're back to people then," said Gideon.

"And two, at least. Not only killin' people, rippin' them apart by hand, but chewing on 'em, too."

That part of it posed no problem for Thorn. He'd dealt with cannibals before and seen one of them hanged before the local law encouraged him to hit the road.

"I meant to ask about a place I passed by, while you were out hunting Wakefields."

"Lotta good it did. Which place is that?"

"I make it five miles west of town, planted in cotton."

"Hell, that's every spread in Chicot County."

"This one didn't have—what do you call them? Overseers? Just a lot of workers in the field, and when a bell rang from the house, they all broke for a drink of water from a wagon standing unattended."

"Right. The boss man there's Orlando St. Germain. Came over from Louisiana, right after the war, and started buyin' land. The Klan talked some about running him off, but since he's not a Yankee carpetbagger and was putting money into the community, my predecessor tried to talk 'em out of it."

"And how'd that work?"

"From what I hear, it didn't. But a couple of the boys in charge—a cyclops, I believe they called one of 'em, and a nighthawk, if you can believe it—up and left the county sudden like, then St. Germain was left alone."

"Is it unusual, his workers being white and black together?"

"Rare, but not unheard of. He got know grief from the Freedmen's Bureau, since he paid 'em all the same. Which isn't much, I grant you, but I guess they sharecrop on the side. You notice something odd about 'em?"

"No," Thorn said. "Nothing that I could put my finger on. You hungry?"

"After seein' Parrot? No thanks. You go on, though. See you later at the house."

Thorn stopped at Johnson's restaurant and had a late lunch or an early supper, call it what you like. The place was short on customers this afternoon, whether because it was an off-hour or people were disturbed about the mayhem overnight and staying close to home, he couldn't guess.

I'm wearing out my welcome, Thorn considered, as the waitress seated him and left him with a menu. *Like I always seem to do.*

The day's special was pan-fried pork chops, two of them, with mashed potatoes, red-eye gravy, peas, and biscuits. Thorn had beer, as had become his practice in Lake Village, and was thankful for the dearth of other diners, whether they were hostile or accommodating.

Afterward, his plate cleared and his bill paid, Gideon walked to the *Sentinel* office and took a chance at finding Ebenezer Gallatin at work. He was, in fact, and had a notebook ready in his hand before Thorn had a chance to state his business.

"I was wondering if you could give me your take on what happened at the Grandee overnight?" the newsman asked.

"Some men came by, hoping to kill me," Gideon replied.

"And...?"

"And I talked them out of it."

"Some talk that must've been. Five dead in town, and one more on the road to Yellow Bayou, running for his life."

"I guess he didn't catch it." Having second thoughts and backing toward the office door, he said, "You'd better ask the sheriff any other questions you might have."

"Did that," said Gallatin. "But wait. Excuse my curiosity, will you? Comes with the job."

"I've worked with news people before. The last one's still missing."

"I'm sorry, but I had to ask. Did *you* have something to ask *me*?"

"I wondered if you know a fellow named Orlando St. Germain?"

"Why, certainly. Successful planters in Chicot County are all well known."

"He does all right with his cotton, I take it?"

"Oh, much better than all right," said Gallatin. "He's had the best yield in the county for the past nine years or so, since buying out the LaPierre plantation, coming over from Louisiana."

"I hear the Ku Klux didn't like him much, to start with."

"Well...you know the Klan. Or do you? Next to coloreds, they dislike outsiders most."

"A couple of their leaders took off, though, I'm told."

Gallatin nodded. "Yes. The rumor was they robbed the local chapter's treasury and found it wise to sojourn elsewhere, while they could."

"The men they left behind eased up on St. Germain?"

"True, but remember, he was *southern*, and presumably a slave owner before the war."

"You say 'presumably'?"

"I tried to do a feature on him when he first arrived. You know, an introduction to Lake Village and all that. There wasn't much to work with—nothing, really, now I think about it."

"Did you think that was unusual?"

"Not really. With so much destruction from the fighting, and courthouses often caught the worst of it, their records burned or looted by..."

"Damned Yankees?"

"Your words, Sir, not mine." Gallatin risked a smile.

"But when you interviewed him..."

"Well, it never got that far," the editor admitted. "Mr. St. Germain's a rather...*private* person, I would say. Keeps to himself for the most part."

"Does all the normal things, though, I expect," said Gideon. "Shows up at church, let's say?"

"I've never seen him there," said Gallatin. "Of course, he might be Catholic. I've never had a cause to stop in there."

"His workers, though. They must come into town"

Gallatin's frown deepened. "Not that I've ever seen, now that you mention it. He has a Negro woman does the monthly shopping for him, buys in quantity. There used to be a chapel out on the plantation, when it was the LaPierre place. Now, I wouldn't know."

"All right then. Thanks again for taking time to fill me in."

"Does your...um, errand...in Lake Village have something to do with Mr. St. Germain?"

Thorn shrugged. "Could be I'll have to ask him that, myself."

"But, as I said..."

"A private man. I understand," Gideon said. "I've dealt with some of those before. One pretty recently, in fact."

"What did you learn from him, if I may ask?"

"Enough," Thorn said. "To satisfy myself, at least. Sadly, he's no longer among us."

Gallatin raised one eyebrow. "Oh no?"

"It happens," Thorn replied. "The gossip was, he disagreed with something that ate him."

TEN

LAKE VILLAGE: MARCH 16, 1877

Gideon and Sheriff Mallory were early risers, both from habit and the pressure of their ongoing investigations. Mutual frustration at the lack of progress on those cases also helped ensure that they wouldn't be sleeping in this morning: Mallory over the Parrot Wakefield killing and his failure to locate the victim's other kin; Thorn at realizing he had come no closer to locating Dinah Pilcher than he was the day he learned that she had disappeared.

At least the sheriff had regained his appetite, and they were waiting when McCallister's opened its doors for breakfast. Diners who arrived later found Thorn and Mallory seated together at a window table and conversing in low tones, seeming as thick as thieves. Most nodded to the lawman, let their eyes skip over Gideon, and once again Thorn wondered whether he was killing Mallory's career.

If so, the sheriff didn't seem concerned.

Gideon had two fried eggs with buttermilk biscuits and

"sawmill" gravy, which turned out to be a thick white mixture that included crumbled sausage, flour, with a hint of cayenne pepper for variety. The sheriff ordered ham, eggs, and pancakes with maple syrup, making up for any lack of appetite he'd felt last night. While chewing, he asked Thorn, "What's on for you today?"

"I hope to have another conversation with Erasmus Jones," said Gideon. "If that pans out, I may stop by a few of the plantations close to town, see whether anyone in charge can spare a little time."

Mallory frowned. "The purpose being...?"

"Dinah left town somehow," Thorn replied. "If she was on the weekly stage—"

"Must've forgot to tell you," Mallory cut in. "I asked about that at the coach line's office Monday noontime, after you came in from your excitement with the Wakefields. Spoke to Truman Chalmers—he's their ticket-taker—and he said she didn't ride with them. I woulda told you sooner, but it slipped my mind, with all the other hoopla going on."

"No problem," Thorn replied. "Unless you've got someplace I haven't found yet, renting buggies out—"

"We don't," said Mallory.

"Okay. Then either someone offered her a ride, or she left walking with her luggage. I can't picture that."

"It's doubtful she'd get far afoot, even without Wakefields to think about."

Thorn *didn't* want to think about them taking Dinah, laying eyes or hands on her. He said, "The only other option I come up with is that she never left at all."

"You think she's still in town? That don't make sense."

"Or someone took her, with her bags, and found some way to hush it up."

The lawman shook his head. I can't see anybody at the Chicot House involved in those kinds of shenanigans."

"Someone from outside, then."

"Would she have gone along with 'em?"

"Depends," Thorn said. "If she thought they had information for the story she was chasing, maybe. If they came on rough, she would've fought them."

"No reports of anything like that," Mallory said, "from the hotel or any other part of town."

"They might have lured her out, then come back later for her things," said Thorn. "The night clerk wouldn't necessarily have noticed it."

"So, you goin' around plantations is...for what, again?"

"If Dinah was taken against her will, she had to be transported somehow. Otherwise, it means she's dead and someone did a better job hiding her body than with Asa Daughtrey's."

"Damn, I hate the sound of this."

"I can't avoid it, though," said Gideon. "If she was carried off, maybe someone at one of the plantations saw something. A buggy passing after dark, whatever it might be."

"And if they didn't?"

"Then my only hope dries up."

"Okay. I know you have to try this, but if St. Germain or anybody else won't talk to you..."

"In that case," Thorn replied, "there's not much I can do about it, is there?"

Pap Wakefield wasn't kidding when he'd told his kin they would be headed back to Arkansas at first light. Mostly riding on horseback, a few women on mules, assorted young'uns in the back of an old flatbed wagon, they were on the road by dawn and crossed the river before any other ferry customers turned out, needing two trips to get the last of them across.

While Pap and Mam were waiting on the Mississippi's western bank, wishing the sun were slower rising so they weren't all totally exposed, Pap finished planning out his campaign of attack. They wouldn't try to strike Lake Village during daylight, which meant lying up somewhere for the remainder of the day, once they were near enough. To reach the kind of swampy hideout they were used to, they would have to cross over some piece of private property in transit, one of the cotton plantations spotted all around the county seat.

Pap didn't much care whose land they'd be trespassing upon, as long as they could get across without riling a foreman in the process, setting off a call to arms. And that put Pap in mind of one place in particular.

One thing he'd learned while still a sprout was that the quickest route between two points might *not* be a straight line. Straight lines often meant sticking to established roads, and that wasn't what outlaws by profession wanted when the law was hunting them, like now.

Pap didn't know who owned the land he meant to lead his kin across, nor did he give a damn. What mattered was a lot of workers in the cotton field but no one keeping eyes on them from horseback and no driver on the high seat of their water wagon. Searching it with narrowed eyes, from well back in the trees, Pap couldn't see the house that ruled them all, its master either safe inside or on some errand, maybe into Lake Village or even farther off. Whichever, Pap believed his tribe could cut across the field and make it out again before a meaningful alarm was raised.

"Can't say I like the look a this," Mam said, half-whispering although none of the field hands were near enough to hear her if she'd spoken in her normal voice.

Pap knew enough to clarify those words before he overruled her, so he leaned in close and asked, "Why not?"

"Don't feel right," she replied, and left it there.

"Don't feel like naught to me," he answered back. "But I can *see* they got no overseers out. We go someplace with guards watchin' the workers, we might have to fight our way across, and there goes the surprise. That's all I need to know."

"Still reckon it's a bad idea," Mam said, then spat tobacco juice into the weeds. "But you's the boss"

That's right, Pap thought, not saying it aloud. *I is.*

He beckoned to the others grouped behind him in the forest shade and started forward on his stolen piebald gelding, knowing that the rest would follow him.

They'd covered thirty yards or so, out into sunlight, when the first field hand glanced up and spotted them. His mouth worked like a fish hauled out of water, no sound audible, but all the other workers stopped and turn to face the trespassers, as if the one who'd seen them first was shouting trumpet-loud.

"Goddamn it!" Pap muttered. Then louder, to his kin, "Get ready for a fight!"

He kept on going, knowing none of them who followed him would have the nerve to cut and run. They trusted him to lead them, and they trusted *violence* as a solution for most problems they encountered, day-to-day.

Pap hoped the field hands would retreat and scatter, but they fooled him, starting forward in a ragged skirmish line, the cotton plants snagging their piss-poor clothes. Most of them still carried the hoes and spades that they'd been using on the rows, although a few had dropped theirs, jogging forward with their scrawny-looking arms outstretched, their dirty fingers hooked like claws.

"Shoot through 'em!" Pap called out, and led the others by example, blasting one of the hands nearest to him with his .41-caliber Colt House Revolver. He saw the worker's left eyeball fly from its socket, which should be killing wound, but it kept charging at him, Mam screaming like someone set her skirt afire, until his gelding brushed on past the dead man stalking and rushed onward.

"What ' hell?" Pap blurted, as he felt fingers gripping his trouser leg and glanced down, where the man who should be lying cold was hanging on and being dragged, his feet scraping across the cotton rows.

And it was then Pap Wakefield showed his yellow streak, whipping his mount around and breaking for the trees.

"Run for your lives!" he shouted to his kinsmen. "Every Wakefield for hisself!"

LAKE VILLAGE

Thorn fetched Shadow from the livery and spent some time with Belle, then rode back to the freedmen's quarter. Shadow knew the way by then, and would've carried Gideon unguided otherwise, but Thorn still kept a loose grip on the stallion's reins, with one hand free to reach a Colt at need.

The quarter's occupants seemed to expect him, or

perhaps they kept a sharp eye out for any white man in these troubled times, when bigots seeking to "redeem" the southern states for white "home rule" cast racial violence in pseudo-patriotic terms. Last year's White House election had encouraged that, both sides appearing eager to abandon freedmen to the mercy of their former owners, and it took a devil's bargain with the Klan for Republican candidate Rutherford Hayes to carry the Electoral College despite losing the popular vote by a margin of 250,000. The backroom deal: withdrawal of all occupying troops from Dixie and tacit permission for white Democrats to deal with racial matters in time-honored fashion, barring freedmen from suffrage and killing them if they "forgot their place."

At least, this time around, some of the former slaves Gideon passed en route to see Erasmus Jones relaxed a bit after they'd recognized him from his prior visit, but a healthy wariness remained. Some of the men kept tools that could be used as weapons close to hand, while anxious women shooed their children off the street and back indoors.

Thorn was a bit surprised to find Jones waiting for him, seated in a rocker on the porch of his unique house, rising only as his uninvited visitor reined in. Gideon sat without dismounting, just in case he was rebuffed this time, but told the neighborhood's de facto leader, "Sir, I'd like to speak with you once more, if you don't mind."

"Only once more?" Jones asked him, not quite smiling. "I suppose you'd better come inside then."

A new addition to the living room's décor turned out to be a wooden crate with chicken wire on top. Sibilant hissing issued from inside, and Thorn stepped close enough to see that it contained four dark, fat-bodied snakes whose gaping jaws revealed pure-white flesh around their wicked fangs.

"Some cottonmouths," Jones said. "You care to pet them?"

"Not today," Thorn answered, "if it's all the same to you."

"You're here about the Wakefields," said his host.

"In part."

"A couple of them stopped by here on Wednesday afternoon, before your fireworks show in town. They took one of our little girls."

"Took her?"

"They didn't kill her, mind. The way they left her, though, it might've been a mercy if they had."

"If it's the pair I'm thinking of," said Gideon, "they've gone to their reward."

"I know," said Jones. "That pleases me, but brings you to your question, seeing one of them got clear of town before he had his...accident."

"Someone played tug of war with him," Thorn said. "He lost."

"I'd say he has atoned. Poor little Parrot. Never knew if he was coming or going."

"You knew him?"

"Colored folk make it a point to know the Wakefields, Mr. Thorn, and others like them. I suspect my people never saw a white man quite like you before."

"Is that a compliment?"

"An observation only."

"As to who or what killed Parrot Wakefield..."

"Ah. The mystery...or one of them, at least."

"I'm thinking they might be related," Gideon replied.

"You could be right. But looking into such things has its risks, as you already know too well."

"My friend—"

"Has passed beyond my sight," said Jones.

"Meaning she's left the area?"

"Not necessarily."

"Well, thanks for that, I guess."

"You have another question, or another part of the same one."

Thorn felt the short hairs prickling on his nape. "I do," he said. "And since you make a point of knowing whites around the county, can you tell me anything about Orlando St. Germain?"

"I know what everybody knows. He came here from Louisiana, early on in so-called Reconstruction. Stories differ as to *why* he came. Some slavers lived like kings before the war, then lost it all—or most of it—from fighting on their own home soil. Some others...well, they may have found it wise to pull up stakes and find a new place to call home."

"And he was one of those?" Thorn asked.

"I know two things for sure. First is, most of the folks he left across the river, white *and* black, were glad to see him go."

"Not popular, I take it?"

"He left...questions."

"Can you elaborate on that?" Gideon asked.

"To pry is dangerous."

"All right. The second thing you know, then?"

"That Mr. St. Germain is not entirely what he seems."

"Sounds like the first thing, turned around."

"Such often is the case in life, I find."

"Okay."

"You plan on seeing him."

"It crossed my mind."

"Take care," Jones said.

"I always do," said Gideon,

Shadow took Thorn back into town, and on from there to St. Germain's plantation, but the stallion wasn't pleased about it. Gideon tried calming him, speaking aloud now that they were alone, but Shadow's thoughts betrayed a measure of uneasiness that wasn't normally like him, even when facing peril at the hands of strangers.

This time, as he neared the spread, Thorn watched out for a driveway leading to the owner's home and followed it beneath a wrought-iron arch whose gates had been removed at some point in the past without being replaced. A double line of weeping willows lined his path, screening the view of laborers and cotton fields from visitors who might've been invited out to some soirée before the Civil War had thrown time out of joint.

The manor house, as Gideon approached it, wasn't what old paintings of the antebellum South depicted. It had once been white, but that was faded now, in need of freshening. Six fat Ionic columns fronting its façade were in worse shape than those outside the county courthouse in Lake Village. Thorn supposed it would've cost a fortune to restore the place—or maybe its new owner simply didn't care.

As he drew closer, Gideon picked up a whiff of gunsmoke on a breeze wafting across the cotton fields off to his left, where half a dozen laborers had paused to turn and stare at him, then went back to their work, as if they'd measured him and saw nothing to fear.

As he drew near, an old black woman—gray-haired, dressed in an ill-fitting satin gown with a hoop skirt—emerged and watched him. Shadow stopped, some ten feet from the porch and wooden steps, before Gideon had a chance to rein the stallion in.

"May I enquire as to your business, Suh?" the woman asked.

"I hope to speak with Mr. St. Germain."

"And you is...?"

Before he could answer that, a voice behind the woman said, "Gideon Thorn."

The man who'd spoken, now emerging from the house, was six foot five or six, dressed all in gray except for a white shirt that had seen better days, as if its last pass through the wash had failed to get it clean. His face was long and sallow, underneath a shock of snow-white that hadn't felt a comb so far today. White sideburns tried to flesh out sunken cheeks but failed.

"I don't believe we've met, Sir," Gideon replied.

"Your reputation rides before you," said the man in gray. "And we've met now, of course. I am the man you seek."

"You've heard about the late unpleasantness in town, I take it."

"Heard? Yes, certainly. As to the purpose of your visit here, I must confess to being at a loss."

"The fact is that I'm looking for a friend of mine who might have passed this way"

"A friend? But please excuse me. I forget my manners. Won't you come inside?"

"Just for a moment," Gideon replied. Dismounting, he looped Shadow's reins over the saddle horn.

"Idalia, call Peter to feed and water Mr. Thorn's fine animal."

"No, Sir, but thank you," Gideon cut in. "Shadow is fine right where he is."

"Shadow," said St. Germain. "A worthy name."

"We understand each other."

"So I see. Please follow me, then, Mr. Thorn."

Gideon gave a parting stroke to Shadow's mane, mounted three steps and crossed the porch, stepping through open double doors into the once-great house.

ELEVEN

CHICOT COUNTY WOODLAND

Pap Wakefield couldn't say exactly when or where he'd tumbled from his horse, but it was long gone, leaving him face down amidst a mass of ferns and wildflowers. He'd lost his Colt at the same time, but somehow hung on to his cane, the only weapon he had left to him except a small boot knife.

Even his hat was missing, not to mention the remainder of his family. He'd heard shooting and screaming as he rode off and left them, Mam included, her cursing a blue streak at him as he left her to whatever doom awaited all of them. He hadn't traveled far, Pap guessed, before he'd turned to club the hungry-looking dead man off his leg, and then a tree branch out of nowhere smacked him in the face, breaking his nose—the third time in his life, that he recalled—and dumping him face-down onto the forest floor.

Suddenly panicked, Pap rolled over, ready to start swinging with his cane again, but could see nothing of the nearly-headless thing that had latched onto him. That was another thing he'd lost, but wouldn't miss it, if the ugly bastard wasn't crawling after him that very minute, gator-style.

He sat up, sharp pain from at least one busted rib making him grimace, which in turn sparked fresh pain from his bloody nose. Blinking, he looked around on every side, but could see nothing of the freak he'd tried and failed to kill.

The hall was that? he wondered, but his first imperative was getting on his feet and out of there as fast as he could hobble through the woods, no destination clear in mind.

It was a safe bet that he'd lost his wife and kinsmen—most of them, at least—but all his ferret brain could focus on right now was Number One. Grieving would have to wait, assuming that he ever got around to it.

And old man couldn't grieve if he was dead, now, could he?

Calculating that he'd lost his local family completely, how many Wakefields did that leave in the world at large? Maybe another ten, fifteen, some of them naught but kids, scattered across three counties, most of the adults in hiding from the law with prices on their heads for this or that they'd done and been identified while doing it.

Live first. Count later.

If he made it through this, Pap could always try to get in touch with the survivors of his bloodline, although how he'd do it was a mystery to him right now. He had no addresses for any of them, and it didn't matter anyway: Pap couldn't write worth shit, and very few Wakefields could read.

That meant he'd have to travel, hunt the others up when none of them were anxious to be found, and tell them what had happened to their kin. Of course, he'd also have to dress it up a bit, delete all mention of his abject cowardice and somehow make himself the hero of the story, fighting to the bitter end until...

Until *what?*

Maybe he'd got knocked out and his horse kept going with him still aboard. Another possibility, he could've fallen in a river and been swept away. Why not, since none of those he told about it would have any clear idea of where the killings had occurred.

Yeah, Pap decided, *that's the ticket. Swept away and couldn't help myself, nor any of the rest.*

No doubt, some of the lesser Wakefields would beg off riding to help him get revenge, particularly with his scheme to raid and sack the county seat by night or day. That smelled too much like pinning targets on their own backs, and one thing that the Wakefield line had never coughed up in abundance was courageous men.

"Take care of first things first," he muttered to himself, then worried someone—some*thing*—might've overheard him, but the woods were shady, calm and quiet, for as far as he could see.

Pap used his cane and an elm's trunk to help him stand. He got his bearings, more or less, though it was hard to spot the sun through all the leafy branches overhead. When Pap thought he was facing east, away from the cotton patch battleground, he started walking slowly, painfully in that direction, putting more ground in between him and the things he had escaped.

And they were definitely *things,* not men, no matter how they'd looked at first.

He'd traveled fifty feet or so before a shadow stepped into his path, coming around an oak's trunk, and two grayish hands shot out to clutch his head on either side, thumbs digging deep into his cheeks. Pap tried to swing his cane, but he had lost the strength out of his arms.

It was astounding to Wakefield, when he heard the wet sound of his own head separating from his neck.

THE ST. GERMAIN PLANTATION

Inside, the mansion smelled musty, its dead air barely circulating, but it seemed to be maintained, if not with loving care, at least something approaching competence.

Two curved stairways flanked the large foyer, ascending to the entry's left and right, both rising toward the second floor's railed landing. From that kind of balcony, two shadowed hallways led back to the rear and out of sight. Downstairs, below the overlook, another corridor passed into shadow, likely granting access to a dining room, study, library, kitchen, and whatever other rooms that rich like his own forebears normally regarded as essential.

"Will you join me in the library?" asked St. Germain.

"My pleasure," Thorn said. "After you."

"Of course. You would not know the way, *n'est-ce pas*?"

"*Bien sûr*,"

"Ah. You speak *français*!"

"Not fluently," Thorn said, "and not for years."

"Perhaps, if you are in the district long enough, you have a chance to practice, eh?"

"Right now," Thorn said, "I'm on what you might call a quest."

They reached the library, passed through its door, and took seats facing one another with a deal table between them. Gideon wished there had been more time to scan the shelves jam-packed with weighty tomes.

"A quest, you say. In search of what, if I may ask?"

"A missing friend," Thorn said.

"A friend?"

"She disappeared from Lake Village some days ago."

"That sounds dramatic: *disappeared*."

"I'm not sure what else you might call it. She checked out of her hotel, not telling anyone she'd worked with in Lake Village, and she hasn't been seen since."

"That *is* disturbing. You must be...beside yourself."

"I'm holding up so far," said Gideon.

"This work your lady friend—you did say 'she'—what was it, if you don't mind saying."

"She's a journalist," said Gideon, refusing to employ past tense where Dinah was concerned. Not yet, at least.

"A story then. Regarding...what?"

"Grave robberies. I don't know if it's common knowledge, but you've had a number of them in the area, and now some unsolved murders, too."

"*Meurtres*! I had no knowledge of them, but I'm seldom in the village and do not subscribe to its newspaper."

"I'm aware of two so far this month," said Gideon.

"Related to the violence in town last night, perhaps?" asked St. Germain.

"One, possibly. The other, very likely not."

The mansion's master shook his head, as if in wonderment. "Such times, we live in, eh? First it was members of the Ku Klux klan dressed up as shabby ghosts, now this. Were they, perhaps, involved."

"There's nothinng that suggests it," Thorn replied. "Right now, I'm leaning toward Voodoo."

"*Vaudou*," his host repeated, with the French pronunciation. "That's extraordinary."

"It's one reason that I hoped you'd speak with me," said Gideon.

"Indeed? You think that *I* know something of such things?"

"I hoped you might, Sir, coming from Louisiana as you do. I understand there's quite a bit of it across the Mississippi."

"I have heard such things as well, but always among *des nègres*. I've never known of any white practitioners."

"Well, it was worth a a shot."

"*Je suis désolé*, Mr. Thorn. If I could help you..."

"There's one other thing," said Gideon. "Another long shot, granted."

"Please, ask it."

"My friend—her name is Dinah Pilcher—left Lake Village as I said, without a trace, no forwarding address. The sheriff says she wasn't on the weekly stage and didn't rent a buggy. With no railroad to the county seat, I wondered...well, if you or any of your staff might recollect her passing by your place, along the road out front."

"And when would that have been?" asked St. Germain.

"Roughly two weeks ago."

"A woman passing by on foot, with baggage?"

"Yes, that's missing, too."

"It would be most unusual. I definitely did not see her, but I'll make a point to ask my workers first thing in the morning."

"Thank you, Sir. That's very kind."

"Think nothing of it. If we can't help one another sometime, in our span of years, what is the point of life?"

"I ask myself the same thing, every now and then."

"Well, if there's nothing else...?"

"No, Sir. I'll get out of your way. No doubt you have a lot to do, running a place this size."

"There's always something," St. Germain agreed. "But many hands make lighter work."

LAKE VILLAGE

Back aboard Shadow and exiting the planter's property, Thorn found the field hands watching him again, distracted from their work although there'd been no trouble at the house. In parting, on a whim, he'd told Orlando St. Germain that he was staying at the sheriff's house in town, in case some passing memory of Dinah might occur to him.

When Gideon got back to town, he got his stallion settled at the livery, assured Belle that there was no cause for fruitless worry—understanding that a part of her mind doubted him—then walked down to the sheriff's office and dropped in on Mallory.

"You need some deputies," Thorn said, by way of greeting, "so you get some time away from this."

"I've got a couple," Mallory replied. "One lives up north in Dermott, near Bayou Bartholomew, by the Drew County line. It's not a real town yet but working on it. And the other one lives in Eudora, covering the county's southern quarter, where it touches Mississppi and Louisiana. Both of 'em have families, and I don't want to drag them in on this."

"That's up to you," Thorn granted.

"What have you been up to?" Mallory inquired.

"I paid another visit to Erasmus Jones and found out that his people had a grudge against Parrot Wakefield for assaulting some young girl before the shootings yesterday. Sounds like he raped her."

"You remember that I run him and his brother outa town that afternoon. Dumb bastards likely figured they should teach me not to mess with 'em. It sounds like Trenton's thinking, picking on a child. Too dumb to know the people from the quarter wouldn't even tell me what went on."

"Jones told me Parrot has 'atoned'. His word."

"You think he was involved in this somehow?"

"I tend to doubt it," Thorn replied.

"So, fill me in on St. Germain," the sheriff said.

"Long story short, he never saw or heard of Dinah. He's familiar with Voodoo, from living in Louisiana, but he's never known of any white folks being mixed up in it."

"That's about what I'd expect."

"You think he'll raise a stink about me going out there?" Gideon asked Mallory. "Speak to the judge or whoever?"

"Doubtful," said the sheriff. "I suspect he thinks we're all beneath him, and there's nobody above Judge Kravitz in the county. Now, he *might* reach out to Little Rock, if he got mad enough. Maybe somebody in the legislature, possibly the governor, if he's got any pull with Bill Miller."

"I left him on good terms," Thorn said, "unless he hides it well."

"Should be all riight, then," Mallory replied. "O' course, you never know with these outsiders."

Thorn smiled at that. "How long does someone have to live around here, before folks accept them as locals?"

Mallory made a thoughtful face and sad, "Not long, considering. Two generations, maybe three should get it done."

"I guess I'd never qualify," Thorn said.

"You tired of Massachusetts? Thinking bout a change of scene?"

"Tired of the road sometimes," Gideon said. "If I live anywhere at all, it's Beacon Hill in Boston."

"Sounds high-toned."

"Pretty much. I never quite fit in. It's more like I fell into it, after my parents died. My father tried to make a break with it in Kansas Territory—eastern Colorado now, since August twelfth—but it broke him instead."

"That's Rocky Mountain country?"

"In the foothills," Thorn replied.

"Still, life on the frontier is hard."

"For those that make it. Anyway, I'm off to supper. Want to come along?"

Mallory shook his head. "I have to sit with Doc Alward and Rosco Cagle, plus our coroner, and see if they have any take on who or what killed Parrot yet. I'll catch up with you later, at the house."

"Sheriff, about that—"

"Say no more," Mallory cut him off. "We still have Wakefields out there somewhere, and I can't have 'em destroying both hotels in town."

Gideon chose McCalister's for dinner and arrived with roughly half the tables occupied. Most of the other customers looked up at him with noncommittal eyes—a victory of sorts, considering the sheriff wasn't with him—but none of them risked a smile. The waitress, trained to please and possibly remembering the last tip she'd received from Thorn, made small talk as she showed him to a corner table, as if this was just another ordinary day.

Taking his seat, Thorn wondered whether Lake Village would ever see another normal day or night again. He hoped so, but as long as there were Wakefields on the loose and someone stealing bodies out of graves—perhaps to resurrect them in some twisted way—he thought the odds were slim to none.

Fried chicken caught his fancy from the menu, served with mashed potatoes and tomato gravy—something else he'd never heard of, but found tasty—and a heaping side of butter beans seasoned with bacon. He ordered beer to chase it all and managed two before he'd cleared his plate, ready to pay the tab and go.

Sundown was creeping in from westward by the time he reached the sheriff's house and let himself inside, using the extra key that Mallory had loaned to him. He'd used the privy and was settled on the sofa when the sheriff entered, finishing a sandwich wrapped in brown paper.

Mallory saw Thorn's look and said, "It's pickled tongue. The butcher makes it and I get a craving every couple weeks or so." When Gideon made no reply, Mallory asked him, "Are you turning in?"

"Guess so, unless you've got something to talk about."

"I wish," the sheriff said. "Still no damned sign of any Wakefields, and the hunt for them's kept me from the families who've had their loved ones... carried off, I guess you'd say."

"No problem," Thorn replied. "I rolled snake eyes all day on this, myself."

"I don't know about you," said Mallory, already headed toward his bedroom, "but I'm gettin' sick and tired of goin' nowhere. What's the point of pinning on a badge, when I can't even solve a crime?"

"I'm betting that you've solved your share," Gideon said.

"Maybe I'll think of something overnight. But right now, what's the diff? Start over in the morning, eh?"

"Sounds good."

Thorn hoped he might fall right to sleep, but soon found that his brain had other plans. He thought first about Dinah, as he had each day since learning of her disappearance—and even before that, if he told himself the truth. From there, his mind turned toward the Wakefields and the local plague of cemetery robberies, mixed up with what he'd learned, or hadn't, from his conversations with Ebb Gallatin, Erasmus Jones, and Orlando St. Germain.

The newsman might be hiding something, but Thorn hadn't caught him lying outright. Was he holding information back, or simply angling for an interview?

Jones had seemed straightforward, but within the limits of what he would ever tell a white man. When he spoke of Parrot Wakefield's "atonement" for a rape, was there a hint of personal complicity?

As for the planter who knew nothing and had seen nothing, well...

An explosive sound of smashing glass, from the direction of Mallory's kitchen, brought Thorn to his feet, six-guns in hand.

TWELVE

Gideon reached the kitchen as three shambling figures—two white men, one colored—burst in through the back-door, ripping one of its hinges from the frame.

Thorn's first impression was that they were filthy: tangled hair, smudged faces, hands, and forearms visible with sleeves rolled up or torn off from their worn out shirts. Their pants fit poorly, sagging on lean hips, held up with knotted twine in place of belts, legs short enough to show him that they wore no shoes or socks on calloused feet with split toenails and grime ground into them.

Their faces, if he'd had to give a split-second assessment, seemed vacant, mouths slack, although their sunken eyes were sparkling bright. One of the white men had a port-wine birthmark on his left cheek, in a roughly crescent shape. None of the home-invaders looked like they were angry, but the way all three of them advanced toward Thorn with grasping hands outstretched told him they'd come to kill.

Drawing his right-hand Colt, Gideon shot the nearest of them—Mr. Birthmark—squarely in the chest. It should've killed him, definitely should've knocked him down at least, but while he grunted and reeled backward for a lurching step or two, he got his balance back and lunged forward again.

While target number one was staggering, Gideon had tried a head shot on the black guy, drilling a .44-caliber hole through his forehead above the right eye. His round punched out the back leaving a trail that looked like barnyard muck instead of blood and brains, and while that enemy had nearly fallen to his knees, he caught himself with one hand braced against the kitchen floot, straightened, and rejoined the advance.

Impossible, thought Gideon, but he was seeing it. And seeing was believing, normally.

Tonight, it might mean getting himself killed.

His third shot, straight into the third man's chest, was wasted like the two before it. Backing off, Thorn tried to think of how he'd stop three men for whom a close-range pistol shot seemed to have no more consequence than a light shove or slap across the face.

While he was backing up, Gideon heard another crash of breaking window glass somewhere behind him, to his left. He pegged it as the sheriff's bedroom window, though he hadn't been inside his host's boudoir. Seconds later came a shot that sounded like Mallory's Colt Open Top revolver, and the curse that followed it told Thorn the sheriff's .44 slug had achieved no more than his.

He had in mind to rendezvous with Mallory in the hallway behind him, leading from the parlor to the rooms in back, but the advance of his three adversaries took Thorn by surprise. All gravely wounded, if you chose to call it that, the trio seemed to pick up speed as they closed in on

Gideon, their dirty fingers flexing now, as if eager to grip and pierce his flesh.

He drew the left-hand Peacemaker and fired both six-guns simultaneously, one more round apiece, none having any more observable effect than his first three. The would-be killers seemed to *feel* the bullets striking them, recoiling from the impact, but instead of crying out in mortal pain, they merely grunted, as he'd heard them doing in the kitchen, when they'd burst inside.

Zombies, he thought, then wondered whether they were even capable of dying. Could a resurrected man be killed a second time? Thorn knew he should've posed that question to Erasmus Jones, but now it was too late.

There were supposedly two kinds of zombies, he recalled: the walking dead, and those rendered obedient by potions. In the latter case, logic dictated that the victims could be slain by normal means. But otherwise...

Thorn bumped against a door jam, backing up, then ducked around it, trying to put space between himself and the intruders while he looked for Sheriff Mallory.

If asked, the sheriff couldn't honestly have said if he was wakened by the sound of breaking glass or by the first explosive gunshot that came after it within another couple seconds, maybe three. At first, he couldn't guess if both noises together meant that Gideon was fighting to defend himself or if a prowler had first cleared a windowframe, then shot Thorn while he slept.

Whatever, Mallory rolled out of bed, roused from a murky nightmare thankfully forgotten in an instant, thrashing at the tangled sheets that tried to hold him back.

Given the state of recent circumstances, his Colt Open Top was lying on the floor within arm's reach, not on the nightstand where he might have struck it with an arm while sleeping, causing it to fall and maybe go off accidentally.

At first, no lamplight he could see by, Mallory picked out the dark shape of a man who'd busted out his single bedroom window and was trying to crawl through it now. He couldn't tell the person's race, or even if he was a stranger, but he seemed damned clumsy in that moment, taking extra swings to clear the window's jagged remnants, then struggling to hoist himself headfirst over the sill.

The figure wasn't saying anything, but rather *huffing* like a winded animal dragging an awkward load. His hands seemed to be empty, and the sheriff reckoned that if he'd been armed, he would be shooting now instead of clumsily trying to crawl inside.

Unarmed or not, Mallory wasn't taking any chances. As he heard more gunshots now, these sounding like they emanated from his kitchen, he snatched up his Colt, cocked it, and took a bold step forward, triggering a shot into the new arrival's chest that stung his ears.

And...nothing.

Oh, the .44 slug hit its mark, all right, and slowed the window-climber for a brief moment, then he recovered, seemed to shake it off, and and finally made it inside, dropping to hands and knees in front of Mallory.

That should've killed him outright, Ethan thought, but it was like he'd barely felt the close-range shot.

Instead of bolting from the room, Mallory stepped closer, bent down a bit, and fired his next shot square into the figure's pate. That knocked him flat all right, but only long enough for the intruder to roll over, sit up straight, and struggle to his feet with one hand clinging to the nearby windowsill.

"Jesus!" the sheriff blurted out. Instead of wasting any more lead on this seeming golem, he retreated from the bedroom, out into the hallway, where he nearly stumbled into Gideon, both of them turning with their pistols raised to fire before they recognized each other from repeated contact in the past couple of days.

"How many in the kitchen?" he asked Thorn.

"Three when I started shooting, but—"

"They won't stay down?" Mallory interrupted him.

"Not one of them. Heart shots and bullets to the head, but nothing."

"Same with mine," the sheriff said. "At least there's only one so far."

"There could be more outside."

"You had to say that, eh? Okay, how do we stop these first, before we worry about that?"

"Head shots don't stop them," Gideon replied. "I wonder how they'd do *without* their heads at all."

As scuffling sounds came to him from the bedroom and his kitchen, Mallory told Thorn, "I've got an axe, but it's out back. The only way to reach it would be—"

"Through the kitchen?"

"Right. Goddammit!"

"I saw a shotgun hanging on the parlor wall," said Gideon.

His double-barrel twelve-gauge, kept for home defense in theory, but out of reach when when indestructible marauders jumped the sheriff in his sleep.

"It's loaded," Mallory informed him. "Double-aught. If I can reach it..."

"Try that," Thorn replied, and as he spoke holstered his

twin Peacemakers. Reaching back, he drew a twelve-inch Bowie from its sheath, a knife that you could use to splinter firewood in a pinch.

"Okay," said Mallory "Try that, but..."

"What?"

"I've got a feeling that we shouldn't let 'em take ahold of us."

"I'm thinking the same thing," said Gideon, and flashed a smile that must've been an effort.

"Right, then. Go!"

Mallory bolted for the parlor, half expecting to find more intruders waiting for him there, while Gideon turned back toward the kitchen.

It wouldn't be the first time Thorn had used his Bowie in a fight against long odds, but he had never tried it on an enemy who seemed immune to pain or crippling injury. What's more, he'd never tried to hack a man's head from his shoulders, much less three of them, while they were working overtime to grab and maybe strangle him.

Still, nothing ventured...and, in this case, failure meant that he could die tonight.

The sheriff sprinted past him, toward the parlor and his shotgun mounted on the wall. Thorn faced the kitchen door and moved forward, both of his pistols holstered now, leaving his left hand free for shoving, grasping, or whatever, while his right wielded the knife.

He kept the Bowie razor-sharp, its weight tipping the scale at one pound and three ounces. If he got the proper angle on a swing, lopping a head off should take two or three good strokes, allowing for the muscles, vertebrae and spinal column, counting on his target to be struggling the whole way through. Whichever one he started with—first come, first served—the other two would doubtless throw themselves into the fight with grasping hands and gnashing teeth.

Their bite was something else he hadn't thought about till now, found only on the dead so far. Was it infectious, like saliva from a rabid animal, or even somehow venomous?

To hell with that. He had to *fight,* and there was no way around it.

The first man-thing to meet him in the kitchen doorway was the black one, roughly Thorn's height, but emaciated-looking, as if he'd been starved almost to death. That should have weakened him, but while the maybe-zombie wasn't fast, he was relentless in his dazed, moaning advance.

Dark hands reached out for Thorn. He batted them aside, one with each of his own hands, then reversed the right-hand swing and slammed the Bowie's blade into the left side of his adversary's neck. It cut deeply, bringing a grimace to that undead face—the first sign he had seen so far of anything approaching human pain—and then the hands came up to block Thorn's second swing.

No matter. It sent severed fingers bouncing on the floor but missed his target's neck and sheared off half its cheek. Wrenching the Bowie free, he had to turn and wake a swipe at one of the two shambling white men, scoring at a corner of the man's slack jaw and causing it to sag off-kilter, yellow teeth exposed.

Shoving that guy away, Thorn turned back to his closest enemy and swung another crushing blow into the neck wound he had opened seconds earlier. His blade lodged in between two vertebrae but came loose when he tugged it hard enough, and one more blow finished the operation, with the head landing between Thorn's feet, its former owner toppling over backwards like an empty suit of clothes.

As Thorn's enemies closed in on him, he heard a shotgun blast from the direction of Mallory's bedroom, followed by the *thump* of something man-sized dropping to the floor. He hoped that it would mean the end of one more trespasser, not simply wasted lead.

Gideon took the fight to his remaining adversaries in the kitchen, both formerly white men, now a pair of filthy scarecrows on a killing mission. One was quicker reaching him, and Thorn was fending off his clawlike hands, seeking an angle on his neck, when Mallory barged in and shouted, "Duck!"

Thorn did his best, before the sheriff fired his shotgun's loaded barrel and second of his shuffling enemies absorbed the buckshot with his face. His skull exploded like a melon packed with fireworks, while the prowler vaulted backward, landing on his back and staying there.

While Mallory reloaded, Gideon moved in, brushing his enemy's right hand aside with his own left, then grabbing a handful of lank, greasy hair. Brown, rotting teeth snapped at him, but Thorn pushed that head back as he swung his Bowie.

One whack, two, and then Gideon was holding up a severed head whose eyes gaped back at him. For a split-second, he thought he must resemble art he'd seen depicting legendary Perseus raising Medus'a head, then he released it as the truly dead man crumpled to his knees, then slumped onto his left-hand side.

Behind Thorn, his reloaded shotgun poised, Mallory

asked him, "Are the bastards dead? Please tell me that they're really dead this time."

The neighbors, understandably, weren't quick to show themselves. Rousted by battle sounds, most of them still in nightclothes, they approached the sheriff's house with trepidation, several of them crowding at the busted-open kitchen door before they dared set foot inside.

"It finished, Sheriff?" asked a portly man who'd thrown a coat over pajamas, taking time to arm himself with a revolver back at home.

"I think so, Paul." said Mallory. "Be careful, all of you, about touching the bodies, though."

"Who'd want to?" Paul replied, but came inside to take a place beside the sheriff's stove.

As more came in, a couple of them women clinging to their men, another said, "Jesus, what *are* those things? They look like men, but..."

"That's the question, Alfy," Mallory responded. "Came in looking dead, they did, but it was still hard work to put 'em down."

A third man hesitantly said, "I hate ta tell ya, Sheriff, but another one just like these got away."

"What? Where?" asked Gideon.

"Comin' across the road, I seen 'im headin' in the opposite direction, back toward Main Street."

"Are you sure, Ben?" Mallory demanded.

"Sure as shit," Ben said, then blushed and added, "Sorry, ladies. Lost my head there for a second."

"Not like these ones," quipped the one named Paul, but no one laughed.

"What did he look like?" Mallory asked Ben.

"Bout like these others, but a white man, more or less," Paul said. "Dirty, but still white underneath it."

"Would you know him if you spotted him again?"

"Be kinda hard to miss, Sheriff. I never seen his face before and didn't think much of it when he passed me. He wasn't movin' that fast, kinda ploddin' like and moanin' to 'imself."

"We need to find him," Mallory advised, but no one moved to follow his advice, while more neighbors kept crowding in, gaping at Thorn, at Mallory, and what lay on the kitchen floor.

Gideon heard the sheriff curse under his breath, with no apology to any women present, then he sighed and said, "Dammit. He's likely gone by now, back to wherever they all came from."

Where they'd come from was the second question on Thorn's mind. The first and foremost behing: who had sent them? He had no illusion that the raiders, in the state he'd witnessed, would be capable of formulating any complex plan themselves, or acting on it.

Stepping closer to the sheriff, Thorn lowered his voice and asked, "Who knew that I was staying here?"

Mallory blinked at him, distracted from his survey of the grisly dead. "Most everyone in town by now, I guess," he answered. "After the Grandee and all...I mean, it *is* the second night you've been here."

"And I mentioned it to St. Germain this afternoon," Thorn said, "while we were talking at his place."

Mallory stared at him. "You thinkin' he—"

Before the sheriff could complete his thought, more townspeople still crowding in, one of the women screamed and slumped against a man Thorn took to be her husband, nearly swooning in his arms.

"Maybe you ladies oughta step outside," said Mallory, "instead of staring at—"

"Jesus!" the fainting woman's man blurted out. "Sweet Jesus Christ!"

"What is it, Ned?" asked Mallory.

"That one," the man said, pointing at the white corpse Thorn had recently decapitated. "That's Eulis, Margie's brother."

"Oh?"

"He's dead," the one called Ned replied.

"Yessir, they're all dead now," said Mallory.

"Nope. He was dead *before*, Sheriff. It's gettin' on three months ago, we put 'im in the ground."

THIRTEEN

The townsfolk kept arriving, drawn by violence and what they thought—or maybe hoped—might be a tragedy. Mallory had to move the ones inside already from his kitchen to the larger parlor, blocking off the broken kitchen door as best he could and opening the front door to all comers who could make the squeeze, repeating admonitions not to handle anything.

More people from the town kept turning up, the new arrivals mostly satisfied to cluster in the front yard or along the street. Exceptions to that rule were Lake Village's two preachers, Father Glover and Reverend Hogan. They arrived together, arguing, and brushed past others waiting in the yard or on Mallory's porch to make their way inside.

As soon as they appeared, Hogan informed the sheriff, "We must see the dead, if you don't mind."

"I *do* mind," Mallory replied. "We've had enough folks traipsing through the crime scene for one night."

"Ridiculous!" the preacher said, turning toward the kitchen slaughterhouse. "I must insist—"

Mallory stopped him with a big hand on his chest. "All due respect, Rev," he announced, "but you don't *insist* on anything tonight. Not in my house, not when it's sheriff's business."

Glover took his pulpit rival's part this time, saying, "Ethan, we may be able to assist you."

"No help needed, Father. All the ones who broke in here tonight are dead."

Glover chimed in again. "But if they were parishioners of ours—"

Again, the sheriff interrupted, saying, "If this lot had come to either of your churches, you'd have called me double-quick."

The preachers both looked equally confused until a townsman standing near them elbowed Glover, saying in a stage whisper, "The sheriff reckons they was all dead when they got here."

"What?" said Hogan. "Clearly, that's not—"

"Possible?" Thorn asked. "Is that your point?"

"It is...unless..."

"Voodoo!" the padre fairly growled, face darkening.

Thorn had to wonder if he'd gone to bed in his black garb and backwards collar, or if he was simply quick at dressing when the sounds of an emergency attracted him. His Baptist counterpart, by contrast, wore a plaid shirt and a pair of khaki trousers that could pass as work clothes on a lowly normal citizen.

The word "Voodoo" was rippling through the crowd in Mallory's parlor, some of them looking like they didn't understand it, others seeming furious or frightened by its sound. One oafish-looking felllow in a corner blurted out, "Voodoo? That nigger witchcraft?"

"Niggers?" echoed someone else.

A third voice issued from a man Thorn recognized, glimpsed briefly in the sheriff's kitchen, saying, "One of 'em were colored. Seen 'im with my own two eyes, I did!"

From there, the racist slur spread rapidly among the all-white locals gathered in the sheriff's living room. One of them took it further, saying to the rest, "That 'rasmus Jones! He meddles in that witchy shit—beg pardon, ladies—over in the freedmen's quarter."

"Jones," others began repeating it, as if they were fixated on some mantra from the Far East. "Jones! Erasmus Jones!"

And when one blotchy-faced, pot-bellied specimen called out, "We gotta get 'im?" no one in the room seemed terribly surprised. Others repeated it, with variations, and a couple of them headed for the door.

"Shut up!" Mallory's voice stilled them immediately, sounding almost like a pistol shot. When they were silent, all eyes on him, Mallory went on. "There'll be no lynching talk in my county. Next one that even hints about it goes to jail for stirring up a riot."

"But Sheriff—" one man started to protest

"Button your lip, Jed," Mallory commanded. "Lynching talk's a misdemeanor that'll get you sent up for a year, whether you're man or woman, and Judge Kravitz will sustain the charge. And as far anybody *getting* anybody else, I promise you the first one tries it, *I'll* get *him* and leave him where my bullet brings 'im down!"

That settled most of them, though Thorn still caught some glaring, and a couple of them whispering beside the street door, heads bent close together.

Something came to Thorn then, and he spoke softly to Mallory, saying, "I just remembered something I should tell you."

"What's that?" asked the sheriff, but he was distracted by two more men coming through the doorway, tellling Gideon, "And here they are. The very people we've been waiting for."

As if on cue, the crowd parted to let the late arrivals pass.

The latecomers were polar opposites: one six feet tall or so, built lean, with a full head of auburn hair topping a weary-looking oval face, his right hand carrying a well-worn leather satchel. Thorn hadn't seen him before. The other one was undertaker Roscoe Cagle, whom he'd met. Both wore dark pants and jackets over white shirts, neither with a necktie.

As the mismatched pair reached him, Mallory introduced the taller one to Gideon. "Gideon Thorn," he started out, "meet Dr. Neal Alward, our sawbones here in town.

Switching the satchel from his right hand to the left, Alward shook Gideon's and told him, "Funny thing. Eight years in practice and I've yet to saw a single bone."

"You shouldn't have to break that streak tonight," Thorn said.

"And you know Mr. Cagle," Mallory went on.

Cagle reached out to shake Thorn's hand again, saying, "The last man who—"

"Will ever let me down," Gideon finished for him. "Good to know, but but I hope that I won't required your services."

Mallory saw the look on Cagle's face and wondered whether Thorn had made an enemy. Before it could sink in, he said, "I've got four stiffs for you to look at, Doc, then Roscoe, they're all yours. This way."

They hit the kitchen first, three butchered corpses lying on the floor. Grimacing, Dr. Alward said, "I'm guessing you already know the cause of death."

"I've got another in the bedroom, came in through a window," Mallory explained. "My first question isn't what killed 'em here tonight, but rather...well, if you think any of 'em died before."

"Before what?" Alward asked, clearly confused.

"Before what you see here, their heads and all."

"Is this some kind of joke?" Cagle inquired.

"Not hardly." Lowering his voice, the sheriff told them, "Ned and Margie Ingstrom tell me this one—" pointing to the last man Thorn had separated from his skull—"is Eulis Brandt, her brother, Ned's in-law."

"My God!" Cagle chimed in. "They're absolutely right."

"And why is that peculiar?" Alward asked.

"Because he fell down drunk and broke his neck back in December," Cagle said. "We buried him two days before Christmas."

Alward asked the undertaker, "Are you sure?" With Cagle glaring at him, he said, "Please forget I said that. Stupid question. Sorry."

"And the question," Cagle said, "is what Eulis and his companions—these two, anyhow—were doing up and on their feet tonight. From what I see at first glance, I would say they've all been...um, deceased...for weeks, and maybe longer."

"What they had in mind was killing us," Thorn said. "I mean, assuming they *had* minds."

Alward, still working through his shock, asked Cagle, "Have you buried either of the other two before?"

"I can't tell on the other white man, since he's got no face. Most of the coloreds take care of their own, according to established custom. The last one I handled must've been a year ago. This isn't him."

"What else can you tell us?" asked Mallory.

"I'd have to make a full examination first," Alward replied, unready to commit himself.

Cagle, despite the weird surprise he'd just experienced, seemed somewhat more assured. "From what I see here, Sheriff, I can safely say none of these three have been embalmed. I *know* the Ingstroms opted to forego it with Eulis. Dust to dust, and all that holy writ."

"The other two?" Mallory pressed.

"Show certain signs of...breaking down, let's say. I wouldn't call it decomposing as we understand it. There's no bloating evident, and no flesh falling off the bone, no maggots or—"

"I get it," Mallory cut in. His stomach felt as if he'd caught it in the act of rolling over, stopping it halfway through the maneuver. "They're not rotting."

"Not externally at least," Cagle replied, and added once again, "from what I see here, almost fully dressed."

"What I wanted to tell you earlier," said Thorn to Mallory. "I've seen the middle one before, just yesterday."

"And where was that?" the sheriff asked.

"Out picking cotton for Orlando St. Germain."

The fifth dead man walking abroad this night is headed home. If asked, he couldn't have explained what "home" meant to him, or exactly where it could be found. He couldn't have said *anything*, in fact, being a mute, not knowing even that his tongue had been removed by someone else's hands.

Still, when he thinks of "home" it draws him, pulls him toward it, like the instinct that makes certain birds fly north or south at the beginning of a certain season, sometimes crossing continents or oceans to achieve their built-in goal.

Tonight, the dead man knows that he has not achieved his goal. With four companions, now cut off from mental contact with him, he'd been ordered by their master to locate and kill a man dressed all in black, along with anybody else who tried to keep them from him. Four had gone into the house selected for them by some means the sole survivor doesn't understand, and now those four were fully, truly dead.

How does the fifth one know that fact? Explaining would've been beyond him, even if his tongue were still intact, his vocal cords not withered like sere weeds baked by the sun.

He simply understands that their master's command includes an order to return, report, and thereby certify a job well done. He's now the only one tonight who *can* return, can pass the information on by some means that he doesn't comprehend.

Together with that order, so imperative, came knowledge that he'd failed to carry out his mission. Still, rather than staying to complete it and, perhaps, to be destroyed himself, he is compelled by the conflicting order to return and to report. Failure to rush inside the house and die—whatever that might mean—was willful disobedience, demanding punishment.

Conflicting orders from the one and only person whom he must obey.

Damned if he does, damned if he doesn't. It is all the same.

And he will certainly be punished for his failure, more severely than he had been other times, for small infractions of his master's laws: breaking a tool at work, failing to meet his daily cotton quota, this or that.

It is a punishment that he both fears and understands abstractly as inevitable, knowing that his master won't be pleased with him.

He won't be pleased at all.

It is the dead man's fault somehow, and without fully understanding why, he willingly accepts responsibility. He lives to serve, if his state of existence can be properly termed *living*. Failure must have consequences, and without his four erstwhile companions, he must bear the brunt alone.

Relief tempers his apprehension as his bare feet touch the soil of home. In darkness, he can't single out a landmark yet, but something in the ground he treads upon feels suddenly familiar. More time slips away, and then he sees the house before him, light showing only in the window of one upstairs room.

Emerging from the woods, he plods across bare dirt, then grass that brushes his bare ankles as he walks across it. Instinct or instruction tells him to steer clear of the front porch with its great colonnade, and so he walks around the south side of the mansion, coming to the service entrance that means access, if the master should invite him in.

He finds the rear veranda, mounts its steps, approaches the backdoor and knocks with all due deference, though loud enough that someone in the house must hear him. moments later, he can see a light approaching from within, an oil lamp carried by his master's hand.

The backdoor opens and his master stands before him, frowning.

"Well?" he asks.

"They failed, Idalia," Orlando St. Germain declared.

"*Les putains d'idiots!*" the old black woman swore in French. "Why did it come back here?"

"My fault," said St. Germain. "Their orders were... ambiguous."

"And was it seen?"

"Not coming home," he said. "In Lake Village, perhaps."

"What of the other four?"

"Dead now."

"*Pour de bon?*"

"Yes, for good. At least, beyond our resurrective powers."

"*Merde!*"

The sole survivor of tonight's grim exercise couldn't communicate by speech, of course. That power had been stolen from him with a scalpel and a surgeon's forceps. Still, what he had seen, experienced, and understood could be extracted from him via laying on of hands, a task that St. Germain found loathsome, even as he deemed it mandatory.

If his activities should ever be exposed, none of the peasants he'd transformed could ever testify against him in a court of law. They likewise couldn't draw or use conventional sign language to communicate. Only by physical contact could St. Germain extract whatever short-term knowledge they'd absorbed through eyes and ears, by taste or smell.

Idalia, who had taught him all those things while they were living in Louisiana, well before the war and other circumstances forced them both to flee, possessed the same powers wielded by St. Germain. If anything, her psychic gifts were stronger than his own.

Which made her dangerous.

Idalia was the only living person who could ruin him—and only then, if stodgy courts bound by their regulations, ruled by simple minds—accepted anything she said as fact. More likely, she'd be lodged in an asylum, if any such institutions had existed in Dixie. Should murder be suspected, it was more likely Idalia would be hanged, her claims against a wealthy white man airily dismissed as lies.

But there was yet another way the crone could threaten him: by turning their creations against him, requiring that they should obey no one but her. By that means, she could have him killed, or possibly transform him into one more shambling thing that did her bidding.

What was stopping her from that so far? She'd been a slave when St. Germain had recognized her powers, rescued her, and granted her relative freedom while it suited him. Without a white master, Idalia's survival would depend on fleeing to a free state in the North, but once there, living on her own, severely limited in wielding her occult strength against enemies or to her private benefit.

America had scrapped its witchcraft laws during the 18th century, but St. Germain knew that there *were* asylums that accepted blacks north of the Mason-Dixon Line, and white lawmen as well, who'd gladly stretch her neck the moment they could prove that she was harming anyone except other...inferiors.

That made him feel secure for now, if only marginally so. Gideon Thorn was still a threat to him, perhaps willing to act outside the law, and if he'd helped the county sheriff in disabling four of St. Germain's creations in a single night...

But he knew someone who might help with that.

"Where are you going?" asked Idalia, as St. Germain began climbing one of the curved staircases leading upward to the second floor.

"I need to speak with her," he said.

FOURTEEN

LAKE VILLAGE: MARCH 17, 1877

Midnight was upon them by the time Mallory's neighbors straggled home. The town's two preachers were among the last to leave, as if both clergymen agreed they'd found an unexpected opportunity to reassure parishioners and those they never saw in church that God still knew what he was doing, come what may.

The last two who remained, aside from Thorn and Sheriff Mallory himself, were Dr. Alward and the undertaker, Cagle. When the rest were gone and those four were alone inside the house, Mallory faced the two professionals and asked them, "Well?"

Alward went first but had little to say. "I'm at a loss," he ruefully admitted. "Anyone can see the cause of death tonight, if that's what killed them. Nobody I've ever heard of can exist without a head."

"I've never heard of anyone who came back from the grave, either," said Mallory. "Unless it was old Lazarus from the New Testament, and I've had trouble buying that my whole life long."

Doc Alward cleared his throat and tried again. "There *are* definite signs of death occurring sometime earlier. How long, I couldn't say. The ones with faces still intact, for instance, all had eyes, not empty sockets, but I poked around inside their mouths as much as I could stand, and none of them have tongues."

"You mean somebody cut 'em out?" asked Mallory.

The doctor shrugged. "It doesn't look as if they rotted out. Beyond that, I can do autopsies on the four of them and try to see what's going on inside, but whether that will fit with anything discovered so far in the history of medicine...I doubt it, very much."

Thorn had been silent up to then, but now he asked, "Could any of them have been drugged," he asked, "to cause a deathlike state?"

"If so," Alward replied, "there's no test on the market to determine it that I know of. And if there were, I wouldn't have the tools to test for it."

"So, we've got nothing," said the sheriff. "Roscoe, will you get your helper over hear and cart 'em off? I doubt that Eulis Brandt's relations will be keen on springing for a second funeral. As for the rest..."

"Of course," Cagle replied. "The doctor can perform whatever tests he wishes, then I'll get them underground as soon as possible."

"And hope they don't come back again," said Mallory.

The undertaker nodded solemnly and said, "Amen!"

Then they were gone, the sheriff turned to Gideon and asked, "What now? Or do I even wanna know?"

"I'm positive the one your people recognized was out at St. Germain's place earlier today. He looked right at me, coming and going. If I'm going to start anywhere, his spread's the place. But first..."

"Uh-oh." Mallory wore a worried face.

"I need to have a last word with Erasmus Jones," Thorn said.

"What for?"

"He talked about two kinds of zombies in Voodoo tradition, one alive and managed with some kind of drugs or venom, while the other—"

"Would be dead men walking, I suppose?"

"Allegedly."

"Well, shit. I'd better go out with you, then, being the so-called law."

"It might be best if you hung back and managed things in town," Thorn said.

"Because...?"

"You may not want to be involved in what comes next."

"With St. Germain, you mean."

"With whoever's responsible."

They stepped outside in time to see a flickering ot firelight from Main Street. It looked like torches, with a background noise of angry voices rising.

"Damn it all!" said Mallory. "I was afraid of this. They're in a hangin' mood."

"And going after Jones, based on the preachers' talk?"

"Down here, don't act surprised. There's not a county in the state that can't claim one lynching, at least." Retreating toward the house, he said, "I'll fetch my shotgun. Do you wanna come along?"

It was the last thing Gideon desired, a last-minute distraction, but he waited until Mallory returned, loading his twelve-gauge. They proceeded to Main Street, and Thorn felt marginal relief when he found Judge Kravitz already there ahead of them, raising his voice to overcome the mob sounds.

"Shut up, all of you!" the jurist ordered. "You know who I am and that I mean what I say. I'm telling you right now, there'll be no necktie party hereabouts tonight. I'm trusting Sheriff Mallory to find out who's responsible for these... events. And when he does, we'll have a trial. If there's a murder case and it stands up, a duly constituted jury will convict the guilty parties. Then, and *only* then, will anyone be stretching rope!"

The crowd of twenty-odd townsmen was rumbling when Mallory and Thorn came up behind them. Shouting to be heard, the sheriff said, "And if the judge's words aren't good enough for you-all, I'll be pleased to shoot whoever tries to override the law. Survivors—and I know you all by sight—will stand trial on a riot charge, maybe attempted murder, and I guarantee you'll do hard time."

That took the wind out of their sales, helped by the sight of Mallory's twelve-gauge and Gideon's pistols. After some muttering to save face, they began dispersing to their homes.

"Well, that was close," said Mallory. "You'd better go about your business, while I have a few words and a couple shots of whisky with the judge."

Thorn fetched his rifles from the sheriff's house, then walked down to the livery. He saddled Shadow, sharing peaceful thoughts to calm the gray stallion and Belle, although his mind was anything but calm as he rode out.

Gideon now knew who was behind the local grave-robbings and other crimes but didn't have a handle on solving the county's problem yet. It shouldn't be that hard to deal with St. Germain per se—if anything, he could lie back and wait to nail him with the Sharps at long distance—but would that end the rash of murders he now blamed on St. Germain's zombies? Or would it only make things worse, leaving a pack of undead creatures like those who'd attacked the sheriff's house at large and on the prowl?

It seemed to Thorn that St. Germain must have some measure of control over his mindless drones, if he had sent a squad of them to Mallory's address in town, but what would happen if that domination was removed?

More to the point, considering his mission here, what did the whole thing have to do with Dinah Pilcher? Would eliminating St. Germain produce an answer to that riddle? Would that kind of vigilante action simply pack Thorn off to prison or the gallows?

Legal punishment wasn't Thorn's first concern, particularly with the sheriff on his side, but if he failed to locate Dinah, whether still alive or dead, could Gideon rebound from abject failure?

Some troubling cases had defeated him, of course, remaining still unsolved. But none of them had touched him personally in the way that losing Dinah would.

"Just let it go," Thorn told himself aloud, as he approached the freedmen's quarter, seeing armed black men step out of hiding at roadside.

"Tha's far enough, white man," one of them warned.

Thorn kept his hands clear of his guns and said, "I need to speak with Mr. Jones."

"S'pose he don't wanna talk wit *you*?" the same man asked.

Somewhere behind their point man, a familiar voice

answered, "Junior, I don't remember asking you to speak on my behalf."

"Nossir," the guard said. "And I 'pologize for that."

Erasmus Jones stepped into view, cradling the shotgun Thorn had spotted in a corner of the living room, on his first visit to the quarter's largest home. Addressing Gideon, he said, "We hear you had some grief in town tonight."

"Word travels fast," Thorn said.

"Those things we talked about before?" Jones asked.

"The very same. They're why I'm here."

"You'd best come on with me, then."

Thorn dismounted, leading Shadow by his reins along the gauntlet of grim faces, weapons poised.

"Another thing we heard," said Jones, "was lynching talk in town."

"The judge and sheriff broke that up," said Gideon. "One of the visitors who came calling tonight was black. One out of four, that is."

"That's all we need." Half-turning toward his fellow residents, Jones said, "You-all keep watch, in case that lynching fever hasn't passed."

At Jones's house, Erasmus led the way inside and set his shotgun on the dining table. "I suspected we might meet again," he said. "I've got a little something that might help you deal with Mr. St. Germain."

"You knew about him all along?" Thorn asked.

"I had suspicions that no white men in authority would entertain, coming from me. As far as proof...something tells me you've seen that for yourself."

"I know at least one of our nighttime callers worked for St. Germain," said Gideon. "I saw him in the field myself, this afternoon. I also know his helpers took more killing than a normal man."

"Because they were already dead," Jones answered, while retrieving a small object from a kitchen cupboard. Coming back to Thorn with it in hand, he said, "This ought to help you. It's a hex bag. Blinds the like of zombies while you carry it, so you can slip right past them with a little luck."

Thorn took the the little burlap bag, tied off with twine, and weighed it in his palm. "What all's inside?" he asked.

"Fixin's," said Jones. "A pinch of graveyard dirt, bone shavings, and an herb or two. With proper words said over them by someone with the power, it should get you past the lookouts. Once you're inside, though...well, most of that comes down to you."

"I saw a lot of people, if you'd call them that, working the fields at St. Germain's place. If they're all as hard to kill as those who came to Sheriff Mallory's, I may not have the strength or ammunition for it."

"Ah. But you don't have to kill them all," Jones said. "Only the one who *made* them what they are today. When he dies, those he's raised should go right back to sleep the way he found them."

"Should?"

"I've seen it work before, but does that mean it *always* will? Who knows for sure?"

"You talked about two kinds of zombies, some dead, others in a kind of trance from drugs or whatever he might have used."

"The maker's poison wins them over, but from there on out," said Jones, "he holds them with the power from inside himself. Get rid of him, that ought to break the spell."

"Ought to."

Jones shrugged. "Again, I guarantee the fixin's in that

bag have worked before, in other places, other times. There's one thing that you should remember, though."

"Which is?"

"Being evicted from your mind and body's just like being turned out of your home. The longer you're away—*adrift,* let's say—the harder it will be for some folks coming back again. Some make it fine, no damage done. Others, it's like they've lost their minds for good. On top of that, if they've been damaged physically in the meantime, they'll come back to a house with broken windows or the roof leaking, who knows what all?"

"You're saying that it's better if they *don't* come back?" asked Thorn.

"I'd never go that far," said Jones. "Just be aware the person who comes home might not be the same person who was sent away."

It seemed a long ride from the freedmen's quarter to Orlando St. Germain's plantation underneath a pallid quarter-moon. Thorn watched the roadside to his right and left along the way, alert for any sign that St. Germain had sent his creatures—his zombies—to guard the road.

None showed themselves or lurched out to attack him as he passed, but that did nothing to relax him. Rather, he became more tense as he approached his goal, trying to recollect how many workers had been in the field during his visit, calculating how he'd overcome them if they rushed at him en masse.

Thorn hadn't tampered with the hex bag he'd received from Jones, just tucked it down into an inside pocket of his frock coat, where he'd have no fear of dropping it should he be forced to fight or take evasive action from his mindless enemies.

But that was wrong, he realized. The zombies weren't mindless, per se. Erasmus Jones had made it clear that their minds—whatever remained of them, once they'd been resurrected or enthralled by drugs—would have been occupied by St. Germain's mentality, his power over them.

Did that mean he could give them orders from a distance, or use them as spies, remotely gleaning information through their eyes and ears? And with their tongues cut out—

That stopped him cold. Would those enslaved by drugs, rather then death, be mutilated by the same cruel means?

His sudden surge of anger made the stallion shy a bit, forcing Thorn to control himself in order to calm Shadow down. It helped, but he recalled his first reaction upon finding out Dinah had disappeared.

And if someone or some *thing* had done her any lasting harm, there would be bloody hell to pay.

THE ST. GERMAIN PLANTATION

"Idalia, we must prepare for uninvited company."

The smile that broke across his servant's face was terrible to see, but not the worst thing that Orlando St. Germain had witnessed in his time. Oh, no. Not even close.

The things he'd seen—and done—would make cold-blooded killers run and hide.

"Is it *him*, Master?" asked Idalia. She sounded hopeful, not afraid.

"It is."

"I hoped it would be."

"After five of our creations went to stop him? Have you lost your faith, old woman?"

It was not from charity that St. Germain had credited Idalia with a role in turning out his force of slaves. When he was but a child, lazing away the hours on his family's plantation in Louisiana, she had taken him in hand—barely a woman yet, herself—and taught him all the rites of Voodoo, pledging him to secrecy with threats that he would be cast out if any other members of his family discovered them. Orlando would become a homeless exile, penniless, while she would certainly be killed for practicing witchcraft.

The secret had been theirs alone, shared in the solitude and darkness, until St. Germain had mastered all of it and she, still passably attractive then, had taught him how to be a man. For that transgression, in and of itself, his father would have had her killed, and slowly, but his family had never known.

At least, they didn't know before it was too late.

He still remembered how they'd screamed when he revealed his power to them, former slaves who had been liberated at gunpoint by Yankee troops, not fleeing the plantation as so many others had, but lining up around the big house to surround it, battering their way inside, annihilating St. Germain's parents, the older sister who had teased him mercilessly all his life, the brutish overseers who were next to useless now, without black chattel in the fields to suffer their continual abuse. Orlando and Idalia had stood and watched while they were torn apart, the bloody remnants scattered, some of them devoured.

In the end, he'd set them free to wander in bewilderment, corralled by the same Union troops who'd set them free so recently. He hadn't known the trick of cutting out their tongues back then, and they talked freely—or at least as freely as their addled brains could manage. When a bluecoat colonel down from someplace in New England heard their babblings, he'd declared them guilty of a heinous crime and had his soldiers shoot the ringleaders, those who were literally caught red-handed. The remainder of them were consigned to serve on chaingangs for the army till they dropped and died.

And in the meantime, with Idalia, he'd headed west.

Not far, of course.

They'd needed someplace with substantial land available, not hard to find under the yoke of Reconstruction. He had spent a goodly portion of his father's shrunken riches on the LaPierre plantation, gone to seed and on its way to utter ruin when he'd come along to save the day.

The new laws, written by Republicans to benefit freedmen—while siphoning substantial income for their Grand Old Party in the process—ordered St. Germain to pay his field hands what was deemed to be a living wage. That hardly mattered if said field hands were not actually *living*, or if those who were—the ones he granted leave to visit town on rare occasions, with Idalia closely watching them —had no complaints about their situation.

And how could they, when they never understood exactly where they were or how they earned their meager living? Truth be told, none of them quite remembered who they were, although he'd left some of the local ones their given names, forestalling pointless questions later on.

If asked by someone like the sheriff, if it should occur to him, those worker ants had a specific script to follow without any deviation. Their master was kind and generous, a cultivated man who understood the changes wrought on Dixie by the war. Of course, he had no grudge against the Yankee carpetbaggers. Why should he? There was enough for everyone and then some, in a reconstructed land.

His workers were the same as they had ever been: illiterate, no bank accounts or other fancy trappings. When a northern teacher came to offer them a mediocre education, all refused her and assured her they were quite content. When spokesmen from the Ku Klux Klan came sniffing around St. Germain, dropping vague threats of harm awaiting him unless he paid them off, they disappeared, pursued by rumors that they'd tapped the order's treasury before they fled.

Scoundrels. And once the sheriff gave up looking for them, feeling no great urge to bring them back, they were forgotten soon enough. Tranquility descended over Chicot County with an end to feuds and other such nonsense although, admittedly, those wars between opposing families provided extra corpses for Orlando's rituals. In turn, when moonshiners aroused the ire of local Christian ministers, his minions had encouraged them to leave they area and brew white lightning elsewhere. As with the pathetic KKK, a few had balked at taking orders from a "foreigner," but those were weeded out, disposed of in the swamp, some of their lesser underlings still picking cotton on his land.

Then came the cursed man in black, brimming with questions no one else but St. Germain could answer, and he doggedly refused to entertain them. Before the stranger reached Lake Village, killing several Wakefields in the process, St. Germain had never heard of him, but in Thorn's presence he sensed power of a sort—not equal to his own, by any means, but still...substantial.

Thorn had witnessed things no other man had seen and lived to talk about. When St. Germain could not dissuade him with denials, he had raised the ante, but that too had failed. Now Thorn was on his way, forearmed with knowledge he should not possess, and he was dangerous.

No matter. He was still a mortal being and would die like any other man, given the proper impetus.

Perhaps with *her* on hand, his passion for the quest might yet be turned against him and become the instrument of his destruction. Thus Orlando St. Germain willed it, and he would not consider any other outcome to their rivalry.

How could a simple living, breathing man defeat him, after all?

FIFTEEN

THE ST. GERMAIN PLANTATION

The hex bag seemed to work as Gideon approached Orlando St. Germain's property. For the last three-quarters of a mile, he'd spotted figures lurking in the roadside shadows, behind trees or shrubbery, and while he kept his Winchester in hand, none of the watchers seemed to see him, rather staring back along the road to town with glassy eyes that never blinked.

How was it possible? Thorn let that question pass, almost afraid of jinxing it if he peeled back the lips of that gift horse to check its teeth.

Besides, he'd seen enough during his time at home with Aunt Drusilla, then long months of traipsing through the West, to know that once your mind was open to outlandish incidents, most anything was possible.

And that gave him no peace at all.

Shadow felt nervous as they passed along the zombie road. Thorn's nose picked up occasional unsavory aromas from the posted guards, and he could only guess what they must smell like to the stallion, with his heightened olfactory powers. In the past, there had been times when Shadow's sense of smell alerted Gideon to dangers that he hadn't spotted for himself, and even though saw the zombies now, he understood his friend's alarm.

Thorn would've tried to soothe Shadow with spoken words but didn't trust the hex bag far enough to count on it rendering zombies deaf, as well as blind. Instead, he passed on thoughts which, although not exactly peaceful, he still hoped might put his mount a little more at ease.

When he could see the manor house by moonlight, Thorn spotted more watchers in the cotton field, standing immobile, covering the driveway to the mansion. As with those watching the road, they made no sound and didn't turn their heads as Thorn and Shadow neared the house.

So far, he thought, *so good.*

Still, Gideon couldn't help feeling that he'd stepped into trap that was about to close around him. If the zombies started moving, he could likely reach the mansion and dismount, send Shadow running for his life while Thorn tried breaking in and searching for the man who pulled their strings, but whether he'd get out alive was an entirely different question.

Fifty yards to go now and tried to sketch his simple plan for Shadow without making any sound. The stallion didn't like it, realizing in his way that Gideon might be embarking on a suicide mission, preferring that they turn around and get the hell away from there.

Gideon thought about dismounting and continuing on foot, but if he took the hex bag with him, would the zombies then see Shadow and attack? Or if he tied the magic bag onto his saddle horn, would they ignore the horse and rush at him?

With no good choice remaining to him, Thorn pressed on. The house loomed over him, a brooding hulk, as he rode past and went around behind it, toward what he assumed must be a servants' entrance at the rear. Dismounting there, he patted Shadow's neck and whispered to him, barely audible, "Be careful, boy."

The stallion stood rock-still in place as Gideon approached the backdoor, tried its knob, and felt it open at his touch.

Idalia was so old that she'd forgotten her birth name. Snatched from her village in West Africa by slavers at the tender age of nine, she had endured the Middle Passage in the hands of sadists, dropped off in New Orleans, where Count Hervé St. Germain had purchased her along with seven field hands, almost as an afterthought or pet to keep around the house. She had received her present name from the master's wife, Countess Lynette St. Germain, and had been called nothing else for the long remainder of her life.

Aside from doing minor chores that escalated as she aged, Idalia—for a time, at least—had served as a companion and playmate for her employers' son, Orlando. They had forged a kind of friendship, or the nearest semblance slavery allowed, while the older daughter of her masters, Antoinette, had been a spiteful, unrelenting bitch to both her sibling and his slave.

But finally, using her memories of Old World magic and the friendship that had grown between Orlando and herself,

Idalia had seen *les baiseurs* pay for all their casual cruelty. She'd forged a life of sorts with the surviving St. Germain, enjoying most of it, but now that life was threatened by a stranger seeking to destroy them both, with all they'd built.

But he would not succeed. Not if Idalia had her way.

She paced the mansion's entry hall, moving from window to window, peering into the moonlit cotton fields. Their guards were all on duty, standing rigidly in place, watching the driveway and the road that carried traffic to and from the county seat. There wasn't much of that, most days, and virtually none by night. Still, she imagined how it might look to the occupants of any passing coach—mush less a solitary horseman—to find scores of mute motionless figures watching from the fields like living scarecrows.

Well, *some* of them lived, still drawing breath and taking sustenance as scheduled, though most were empty husks of men and women, occupied and animated by her master's will.

As he had learned from her over their years together.

All that St. Germain knew of the dark arts, she had taught him. But, of course, she hadn't taught him everything *she* knew. If need arose, she always had a few surprises left.

Much like the short double-edged dagger that Idalia gripped in her right hand, prepared to fight at that level if necessary, should her magic fail.

But *could* it fail? When had that ever happened in the past?

Never.

All she lacked now, as time advanced upon her, was eternal life. And with her power to inhabit other vessels, occupy them like mere clothing with her mind and memories intact, why should that threshold of achievement prove intractable?

A sudden twinge of almost-panic sent a shiver down Idalia's spine. Something was wrong, but what?

She started checking windows once again, confirming that their sentries had not budged, but the uneasiness remained. In fact, she felt it growing worse.

How could this happen? How could the upstart visitor have penetrated her defenses without being spotted by the lookouts, mobbed and taken down? They had strict orders not to harm him fatally, at least until he'd been interrogated by Orlando and herself, but now...

Impossible, she thought. *It couldn't be.* Unless...

Was someone helping him?

Idalia's mind flashed to a dark face she had seen on more than one occasion, wondering if *his* powers were strong enough to merit intervention. She'd foregone that pleasure, in the knowledge that a wise man—and he did seem wise—would be content to close his eyes, leave well enough alone.

Had he betrayed her now?

Picking a staircase, rushing upward, she called out to St. Germain, "Master! Orlando! He is here!"

Inside, the house was silent as a tomb, but that was little consolation when the dead could manifestly rise and walk abroad to maim the living. First thing through the backdoor, Gideon came face-to-face with a zombie—another white man, though you had to search through layers of dirt to verify it—and the thing stared blankly at him, through and past him, without seeming to observe him.

So the hex bag was still working.

As a hedge against the zombie's other senses, Thorn left the backdoor standing ajar, afraid to shut it lest the noise might set its watchdog off and make him charge. Holding his Winchester dead-level on the creature's flacid face, Gideon moved around the thing almost on tiptoe and proceeded toward the double set of stairs.

The nearer of them was the left-hand staircase. Gideon surveyed the entry hall, sweeping his rifle's sights across two zombies standing at the tall front windows, staring placidly into the night beyond. When neither of them registered any reaction to his presence, Thorn began ascending toward the second floor, his every sense on full alert.

And suddenly, as if from nowhere, St. Germain's black maid, housekeeper, whatever she was, appeared before him on the second-story landing. She was standing oddly, right hand tucked behind her back, leaving no doubt in Thorn's mind that she carried some kind of weapon hidden there.

Smiling, wearing a grim expression that he could've done without seeing, she asked, "You sure you want to be hee, Sonny? Are you *really* sure?"

"As sure as sure gets," Thorn replied.

"You know our secret, eh? At least a little of it, *pour vous attirer*?"

"I'm not enticed by anything I see here, Lady. Try *repoussé*."

"Honestly?" she answered. "Are you so repulsed, *Monsieur*? Not even curious a little bit about raising *cadavres* from their graves to live again and do your will?"

Thorn climbed another step, then two. "Nothing that I've seen looks like living. There's a time to lay it down and let it go."

"*Oh oui*? And is your time to lay it down, as you say, possibly tonight?"

Her right hand eased into the open, as he'd thought, clutching a wicked-looking knife.

"You bring a knife to a gunfight? I would've given you more credit for intelligence than that," Thorn said.

"But this is not a fight, *cherie*. It is an execution. Yours."

"I don't like killing women," Thorn cautioned. "No matter what they've done."

"But you don't say you haven't done it, eh? And might again?"

"You're foolish, testing me."

"But only if I lose," she said, and then her hand flicked forward to release the dagger, flashing as it spun end over end to strike him low down on his side.

It hurt but didn't spoil Thorn's aim. He put a .44 slug through the crone's chest, slamming her down backwards on the steps. She bounced once, slid two risers downward, closer to him, then lay still. Her jaw was slack, her eyes already glazing over as Thorn plucked the dagger from his flesh and flung it from him, after checking first to see its blade wasn't discolored by some potion that would go to work inside him.

On the landing up above, a man's voice bellowed out in anguish. Glancing up there, Gideon beheld Orlando St. Germain clutching the banister, as if to keep his balance, wild-eyed, red-faced in apparent grief.

St. Germain felt icy fingers close around his heart and squeeze, a pain like nothing he'd experienced since childhood and had duped himself into believing he would never feel again. The grisly vision of Idalia sprawled across the stair below him, dark blood welling from a wound between her breasts, felt much as St. Germain imagined that his own death throes might feel.

"*Bon sang, monsieur*!" he shouted at her murderer. "Goddamn you, Sir!"

"Which god would that be?" Thorn replied, stepping around Idalia's body as he moved closer to St. Germain. "One of your pet orishas? Maybe Ogun? How about Shango or Yemoja? And what about Oranyan or Ibeji? Pick your poison, St. Germain."

"You dare profane their names, blasphemer? Any one of them could crush you like an insect, and I have four hundred at my beck and call!"

"So, call them then," Thorn mocked him. "Go ahead. From where I stand, you seem to be a little short of allies."

"Am I, really?"

Thorn turned back to check the window-watchers in the entry hall, but neither of them had turned toward the sound of gunfire. What on Earth was wrong with them? Orlando reached out to them with his mind, so full of rage, and in return felt...nothing.

"You suppose that you can undermine my power in my own house, *fils de pute*? Are you that devoid of intellect?"

"I'm doing all right so far," Thorn replied, and mounted two more steps. The muzzle of his Winchester was locked on target, one of Gideon's dark eyes sighting along its barrel toward Orlando's heart.

"You think I've come unarmed?" asked St. Germain. "How did you put it when you killed Idalia? 'Bringing a knife to a gunfight'?"

"Her last mistake," said Thorn. And moved another step higher.

"Then feast your eyes on *my* weapon, pathetic unbeliever! This is what you wanted, *non*?"

He snapped his fingers, heard and felt the woman moving up behind him, stepping past him, staring down at Thorn, pausing at St. Germain's elbow.

"Well, *Monsieur* Thorn? Is this who you've been searching for?"

Beside him, Dinah Pilcher, brandishing an axe in her slim hands, told Thorn, "I've missed you, Gideon."

Gideon gaped at Dinah, standing on the topmost stair above him, next to St. Germain. She wore a floor-length gown he'd never seen before, with low-cut bodice and a silken scarf around her neck. The axe she held in a two-handed grip resembled something lifted from a suit of armor in Medieval times.

"Dinah?" he asked, unable to believe it at first glance. It seemed to Thorn he might be dreaming, never mind the sense of warm blood near his waistline.

"You came looking for me, Gideon," she answered back. Her voice was softer than he had remembered, almost dreamy, but at least she *had* a voice. Whatever else she'd suffered in the past two weeks and change, she hadn't lost her tongue.

"As soon as I found out," Gideon said.

"*N'est-ce pas comme ça*?" said St. Germain, mocking. "Isn't this touching?"

Thorn's voice was as cold as glacial wind when he said, "Tell me what you've done to her."

St. Germain grinned down at him, barking a hollow

laugh. "What have I done? The question should be what have we *not* done in out short time together."

Studying the older man over his rifle's sights, Thorn kept his mouth shut, waiting.

And it seemed that St. Germain could not abide the silence. "Most of my creations, as you've seen, are simply silent and obedient. Not this beauty, I'm pleased to say. It was a challenge to subdue her will, of course. I had to use more drugs than usual after she stopped for tea and questioned me about the grave-robbings. But once under control, she has been...*magnifique*. You found her thus, yourself, *n'est-ce pas vrai*?"

It *was* true, but Thorn wouldn't take the offered bait, refused to picture Dinah in this monster's arms. That would come later, if he managed to survive the night. Instead, his mind locked onto trivia.

"How did you get her things from the hotel?" he asked.

"Child's play," said St. Germain. "I sent Idalia to the Chicot House with one of my creations, on the first night darling Dinah spent under my roof. The zombie proved unnecessary. The night clerk enjoys whisky. There was no need to kill him."

"And she's been here all this time," Thorn said, not asking him.

"*Bien sûr*. Of course. Why would I ever let her go?"

"She's going now," Thorn answered. "One way or another."

"Is she? Shall we let Dinah decide?" Placing a hand on Dinah's shoulder, St. Germain told her, "He plans to murder me and kidnap you. See what he's done already to our poor Idalia."

Dinah's eyes shifted from Thorn's face to the old black

woman's corpse. Her voice was furious as she said, "Murderer!"

"And worse than that," said St. Germain. "He would destroy our perfect life together."

This time, Dinah didn't speak. The sound she uttered was a feral growl.

"You call this slavery a perfect life?" Thorn challenged him.

"For me, at least. For Dinah...well, she'll never know the difference."

"Bastard!"

"I was not, in fact," said St. Germain. "My parents married in the Holy Church and bore another child before me. I believe you mean to say *connard,* or possibly *morceau de merde.* I could not, in good conscience, contradict you."

"Come on with me, Dinah," Thorn said.

"Will you go with him, *mon plus cher*? And if not, what should we do with him?"

"Cleave him!" Dinah replied, her face and voice almost hysterical, a lightning change.

"By all means!"

Snarling, Dinah raised the axe and started down the stairs toward Gideon. For his part, Thorn aimed past her, to her right, and fired his rifle for the second time tonight.

The bullet punched through St. Germain's forehead, dead center, spraying crimson out the back, his gray hair listing like a sun flap on the caps worn by French Legionnaires before he toppled over backward, all but his scuffed boot soles out of sight.

Behind Thorn, thumping sounds distracted him from Dinah. Knowing it might cost his life, he half-turned from her, finding that the window-watching zombies had collapsed.

A stifled cry from Dinah brought him back around, seeing her drop the axe, hands raised as if to shield her face as she collapsed and plunged headlong downstairs. Thorn dropped his Winchester and caught her, ready to restrain her if she struggled, but she'd gone limp in his arms. He thought she might have fainted, when she looked up to his face, meeting his gaze.

"G-Gideon?"

"Come on," he said, while lifting her. "We need to get away from here."

EPILOGUE

LAKE VILLAGE: MARCH 17, 1877

"And then the house just...what? Caught fire all by itself?" asked Sheriff Mallory.

"Best guess," Thorn said, "I think one of the zombies knocked a lamp down when it fell over."

"Zombies. I swear to Christ, I never wanna hear that word again."

"I know the feeling."

"Okay. You put down St. Germain in self-defense and then...what? All the things he brought to life died with him?"

"As predicted by Erasmus Jones."

"That one knows too much for his own good, if you ask me."

"I owe my life to him," Thorn said. "And Dinah's, too."

"I know. Still, it could be a chore to keep some of the rednecks off his back."

"I'm trusting you can handle it, Sheriff."

"I'd like to think so." Sounding hesitant, Mallory asked,

"This dropping dead thing—going *back* to being dead, I mean—has that eliminated all the bodies he dug up?

"It should have," Thorn replied. "As we were leaving, they were lying all around the house and in the fields, along the road."

"I mean the ones that aren't accounted for, like them that murdered Asa Daughtrey and Parrot Wakefield. How far did the message or whatever you'd call it reach when St. Germain went down?"

Thorn shrugged. "You'd have to ask—"

"I know. Erasmus Jones."

"One more reason to keep him safe and sound, in case you need him somewhere down the road."

"About these folks we found walking out there, like they were in a dream..."

"The ones who St. Germain trapped with his drugs and poisons," Thorn replied. "Depending on how long he had them under his control, and what they suffered physically, they should come back around in time."

"Sounds like Doc Alward will be busy for a good long while. And I'll be busy trying to find out where they belong, if they can't tell me. Damn. I wish we had some kind of file on missing persons."

"I can't help you there," said Thorn. "I'd have to guess that they were travelers who came along from time to time, and St. Germain thought he could use more help around the place, maybe some workers who seemed human, just in case somebody started asking questions."

"The good news is, a couple of 'em are already talking. Not too clear on who they are or where they come from yet, but both of 'em recall a fight with what they call a pack of 'hillbillies' or 'shady characters' a couple days ago."

"And what became of them?" asked Thorn.

"It's more what *they* became."

"Dinner?"

"*Bon appétit*," said Mallory.

"Wakefields?"

"That would be my surmise. Keeping my fingers crossed."

"Can't say I'm sorry for them," Gideon replied.

"And what your...newswoman?"

"I've made arrangements for her with my oldest friend. She'll be recuperating at a private hospital, McLean's, in Charlestown, two miles north of Boston. They take care of special patients and they have a sterling reputation. Hopefully, all Dinah needs is rest and help to talk through all that's happened to her."

"You'll be going with her?"

"I'll be taking her to Little Rock. We'll find a private nurse who won't mind traveling a bit. They'll catch the train from there, and she'll be met in Boston. My friend's taking care of the arrangements as we speak."

Thorn had dispatched a wire to Boston when the local Western Union office opened. Leaving out the details, he had told Obi Magoro that Dinah needed his help and that Thorn would be covering the cost. His Aunt Drusilla's contributions to McLean's Hospital ought to pave the way, and Obi would be checking in on Dinah regularly, taking no guff from the staff, till she was fit to travel on her own again.

Or she could stay on Beacon Hill a while, if that suited her better. Thorn might see her there, unless some other urgent matter kept him in the West and on the hunt.

"And does she know this friend of yours?" asked Mallory.

"They're more like family," said Gideon. "They saved each other's lives a few months back, and mine as well."

"Another job like this?" the sheriff asked.

"Nothing like it," Thorn said. "But finishing it felt about the same."

"You lead a strange life, Gideon," said Mallory.

"Tell me about it," Thorn replied. And laughed for the first time he could remember in the past two weeks.

A LOOK AT RIP TIDE BY MICHAEL NEWTON

Gideon Thorn returns in a deadly hunt along the Mississippi.

When a paddle steamer is torn apart by an unseen force on the Mississippi River—leaving only one survivor—newspaper reports of the massacre stir Gideon Thorn into action. Drawn to Natchez by the scent of blood and mystery, Thorn faces his most elusive quarry yet: an aquatic predator capable of destroying ships and devouring crews without a trace.

But the monster in the water isn't the only threat lurking in Mississippi.

Navigating the treacherous racial politics of the post-Reconstruction South, Thorn uncovers a town rotting from within. Freedmen fight for dignity in a white supremacist stronghold still bitter over losing the Civil War. As Thorn digs deeper, confronting both ancient terror and modern hatred, he finds himself walking a razor's edge between predator and prey, justice and vengeance.

Rip Tide is a pulse-pounding fusion of Southern Gothic horror and supernatural frontier adventure...where even the river runs red.

AVAILABLE MARCH 2026

THANK YOU

Thank you for taking the time to read *Empty Graves*. If you enjoyed it, please consider telling your friends or posting a short review. Word of mouth is an author's best friend and much appreciated.

Thank you.
Michael Newton

ABOUT THE AUTHOR

A California native, Michael Newton published over 215 books under his own name and various pseudonyms since 1977. He began writing professionally as a "ghost" for author Don Pendleton on the best-selling Executioner series. With 104 episodes published to date, Newton nearly tripled the number of Mack Bolan novels completed by creator Pendleton himself.

www.ingramcontent.com/pod-product-compliance
Lightning Source LLC
La Vergne TN
LVHW040218110826
845146LV00005B/1341

* 9 7 9 8 8 9 5 6 7 6 0 9 7 *